To Josh!

I SPY

Hope you enjoy
the journey!

To Julia and Hatijeh, the best of friends

My thanks also go to The Triumvirate:
Jenny, Megan and Rebecca – without whom
all this would not have happened

First published in the UK in 2009 by Usborne Publishing Ltd., Usborne House, 83-85 Saffron Hill, London EC1N 8RT, England. www.usborne.com

Copyright © Graham Marks, 2009

The right of Graham Marks to be identified as the author of this work has been asserted by him in accordance with the Copyright, Designs and Patents Act, 1988.

The name Usborne and the devices ♀ ⊕ are Trade Marks of Usborne Publishing Ltd.

Cover illustration by Mick Brownfield.

This is a work of fiction. The characters, incidents, and dialogues are products of the author's imagination and are not to be construed as real. Any resemblance to actual events or persons, living or dead, is entirely coincidental.

A CIP catalogue record for this book is available from the British Library.

JFMAM JASOND/09 92032 ISBN 9780746097106 Printed in Great Britain.

I SPY

THE CONSTANTINPOLE CAPER

A STORY OF ESPIONAGE AND ADVENTURE

GRAHAM MARKS

USBORNE

1 21.44, 15TH AUGUST 1927, PARIS

T. Drummond MacIntyre III, son of T. Drummond MacIntyre II (Senior Vice President of MacIntyre, MacIntyre & Moscowitz Engineering, of Chicago, Atlanta and New York City), sat on a bench, trying his best to give the impression he had his nose in the most recent copy of *Black Ace* magazine – if there was anything better to read than detective fiction, he had, in his opinion, yet to find it.

As he pretended to read he kept his eyes peeled for the man he'd spotted. The man, wearing a sharply-tailored, black double-breasted suit and a dark grey fedora, who also had a pencil mustache...and who he was *sure* he'd seen on the boat train *and* at the station in London.

Each time he'd noticed him, the man had turned and, like a shadow, slipped out of sight. He was *sure* the guy was following them, but why he'd follow him and his father he couldn't figure out. His pop helped *his* pop, Gramps, run the family company, which made machines which made machines. That kind of thing. He was *not* the kind of person who got followed by men in dark grey fedoras; unfortunately, in Trey's opinion.

Aware of exactly, word for word, what his father would say to him if he left the bench to investigate these curious circumstances, Trey gritted his teeth and stayed put. He could solve this mystery, if only he was allowed to, but his father was no fan of his ambitions to be a private eye, or of *Black Ace*, for that matter, and would no doubt confiscate the magazine, given the opportunity. So he actually did start to read, which was no hardship as there was the second part of *The Snarl of the Beast*, a Trent "Pistol" Gripp story, in this issue. And Trent Gripp was the bee's knees when it came to sleuths and gumshoes, the kind who generally always shot first and hardly ever bothered to ask questions later...

* * *

"Time to go, son!"

Trey looked up to see his father as he *marched* past him across the concourse of the Gare de Lyon, making for the platform where the Simplon *Orient-Express* was waiting to depart on its journey to Constantinople at 22.20 sharp.

T. Drummond MacIntyre II was in something of a hurry, and it showed; there was a schedule to keep to, his ramrod posture and clicking heels seemed to say, and by heaven that was what was going to happen! Some holiday *this* was turning out to be, was all T. Drummond III (generally known by one and all as Trey) could think.

This trip had been sold to him by his mother as "a golden opportunity" to spend some time with his father on an "educational holiday", and if you wanted his opinion, Trey MacIntyre had more than somewhat been sold a pup. For a start there was no such animal as an "educational holiday" because, as anyone with half a brain knew, a holiday was time *off* from education! But Trey had been prepared to let that point go as he really was looking forward to being with his pop. Except that everywhere they went his father always seemed to have business that just *had* to be done – telegrams to pore over, wires to send, phone calls to take and make, letters to write and people who demanded to be met.

So, while his mother did whatever it was you did when you visited friends in Bel Air, California – his parents did not normally have separate holidays, but, as his mother claimed to get seasick in the bath, a trip across the Atlantic was never going to be on her agenda – Trey had travelled first by train from Chicago to New York. Here, at the window of his father's office suite in the Woolworth Building ("The tallest building in the world, son, all 792 feet of it!") he had watched, boggle-eyed, as thirty-three floors below, Broadway was turned into the Canyon of Heroes by the incredible ticker-tape parade – a sight he'd only ever seen before in smudgy newspaper photos – for the heroic flyer Charles Lindbergh. It was hard to make out much through the blizzard of thin strips of newsprint streamers being thrown out of windows, but he had *personally* seen the very first man to fly solo across the Atlantic! Now *that* was what he called an educational experience!

From then on, apart from the sea voyage, First Class, over to Liverpool, England, on the RMS *Aquitania* – five *days*, and some, which was rather more than Mr. Lindbergh's thirty-three and a half *hours* to Paris – the holiday had settled into a somewhat duller pattern. He had been taken on a car trip round various Scottish castles – Scotland being the land of his forefathers, as he'd constantly been reminded by his actual father.

From Edinburgh ("the Athens of the North, son, the Athens of the North", which didn't, thought Trey, say much for Athens itself) they'd gone on to visit London (rainy) and had taken the boat train over the Channel to Paris (also rainy, but with garlic and bad plumbing).

And everywhere they went there were always meetings, meetings, and yet more meetings (who knew engineering was so much about talking and not about making things?). But maybe, thought Trey, as he stopped while his father instructed the porters which of their trunks were to go to the compartment and which to the baggage car, the same would not be the case while they were on this part of the trip. No telephones, no colleagues, offices or business to do on the Orient Express...and hopefully the food would be better than the frankly dull stuff that had been served up in a lot of the swanky hotels and houses they'd stayed at. Most of the restaurants his father liked to eat in never, ever served ketchup or proper yellow mustard, let alone a hamburger and French fries, or a hot dog and onions, to put them on.

According to the man from Thomas Cook, this trip to Constantinople ("Where the East meets the West, Mr. MacIntyre – two continents in one city!") should take them about a week, all being well. Trey had no idea why the original itinerary (a rather dull-sounding trip to the Côte d'Azur, with visits to a bunch of vineyards, then back to London via Paris) had been changed, but figured it had to do with business (what, in his father's life didn't?) and he had to say he'd no complaints as this new route did sound a lot more exciting. The map that Trey's father had given him showed they'd be going from Paris to Lausanne, in Switzerland, then across the border into Italy and on to Milan and Venice, where they would be stopping for a day or so.

"'Though there are some disagreeable things in Venice,'" his father had told him the night before, smiling as he read from a book, *"'there is nothing so disagreeable as the visitors'*! Henry James said that..."

Trey had no idea who Henry James was, and the information served only to make him wonder why his father was so keen they should go to Venice, and what other unpleasantness might be waiting there for them once they arrived – more than likely *more* museums, galleries and theatres, of which he'd seen enough to last a lifetime, to his way of thinking.

After Venice they still had the cities of Belgrade and Sofia to pass through before reaching their final destination, and all Trey hoped was that, if the journey ended up turning out to be a bore, his father wouldn't stop him from reading his magazines. He'd brought a number of them with him, in fact almost enough to fill one of his cases, all of which his father regarded as worthless trash.

"Trey – stop daydreaming and get on board, son!"

Trey looked up and saw his father calling over his shoulder to him from the steps leading up into the gleaming blue carriage; as he began to follow him onto the train an odd feeling that he was being watched made him turn round, and what he saw stopped him dead in his tracks...the man was there again, some little way down the platform, staring right back at him, his dark, slitted eyes flicking from him to his father!

"*Trey!*" his father barked.

Quite sure that Trent Gripp would have been straight up the platform to find out who the man was and why he'd been putting the eye on him, Trey, on the other hand, had no option but to do as he was told...

2 THE ORIENT EXPRESS

At precisely 22.20 the train heaved itself into motion, the start of the journey heralded by a lot of clanking and the screeching of steel on steel as the wheels bit on the rails, all accompanied by the slow but steadily building pulse of the massive steam engine up front. As soon as he could, Trey got out of their fully-appointed sleeper compartment, which was situated towards the front of the train, and set off to explore the rest of the carriages. At least that's what he told his father he was doing.

What he was *actually* up to was trying to find out if The Man With the Pencil Mustache (as the story would be called if it was in *Black Ace* magazine) had got on the train with them. And if he had, was he following them? And *if* he was – why? These questions demanded to be answered and Trey figured that this was a very good time to do some snooping, when everyone was, like his father, trying to sort themselves out – searching for misplaced luggage, remembering what they'd left behind and complaining about their accommodation to the harassed steward; under these circumstances, no one was going to pay too much attention to some kid.

The first thing Trey noticed was that, unfortunately, there were a few other kids around his age on board, which meant he was probably going to have to put up with his father trying to make him get to know them. Even if they didn't speak a word of English. Which, seeing as they were in *France*, for heaven's sake, was highly likely. And he did not need any new friends, especially ones chosen for him purely by circumstance, something his father consistently failed to understand.

Pushing on, Trey made his way towards the rear of the train. Monsieur Mustache, as Trey now thought of him, was nowhere to be seen in any of the sleeping compartments ahead of the dining car (although a lot of them did have their doors shut, and he made a note

of which they were so he could check them out later);
the mystery man wasn't in the dining car either, which
wasn't altogether a surprise as they weren't actually
serving food yet, so Trey carried on with his search.

Eyes peeled, he sauntered along the gently swaying
corridors, the engine picking up speed as they began to
hurtle through the night towards Switzerland, and by
the time he'd reached the baggage car there was still no
sign of Monsieur Mustache. Trey was sure he'd been
as dedicated and professional a snoop as any of the
gumshoes he read about, which meant that the man was
either in one of the cabins he'd not yet seen the inside
of, or – and he really did *not* want to consider this
possibility, but knew he had to – maybe the man hadn't
got on the train and had never been following them in
the first place.

Trey, shoulders slumped, was just pondering this
thought when the door next to him, which led to the
baggage car, opened and a man came out. He was
dressed in a black double-breasted suit, had on a dark
grey fedora and sported a pencil mustache and Trey was
so glad to see him he almost cheered out loud.

"E'scuse me," the man said, in an obviously foreign
accent; he smelled of heavy, dark tobacco and cologne
and his black hair, Trey noticed as he went past, shone
with pomade like it had been polished.

He hadn't given Trey a second look...but did that mean the man was just not repeating the mistake he'd made on the platform when he been spotted staring, or that he really *didn't* give a darn?

Letting the man have half a carriage start, Trey began to follow to see where he went and whom he might talk to, traipsing behind him until the man stopped by a carriage exit door; he lit a stubby, yellow cigarette with a match and stared out at the passing night, the pungent smoke drifting down the corridor. Trey hung back, racking his brains trying to think what to do next – mooch around and try to appear like he was supposed to be there? Walk on past Monsieur Mustache?

And then a hand gripped his shoulder, and he froze...

"Monsieur MacIntyre? *Votre pere...excusez moi...* your father, 'e is looking for you, young man."

Trey turned round and saw one of the conductors looking down at him. "My father?"

"*Exactement,* 'e was worried, telling me you 'ave been *quelques minutes...*some time." The man examined his fob watch as if to emphasize the point, and then made a shooing motion with his hands. "*Il attend...*'e is waiting for you in the restaurant car. You 'ad better go."

Trey nodded, mumbled a "*Merci, Monsieur*" and then, as the conductor walked away, he saw that his target had disappeared! Resisting the urge to run, Trey walked as fast as he could, desperately trying to catch sight of Monsieur Mustache. He was nowhere in sight, but as Trey hurried past one particular cabin, cursing his luck and the conductor's bad timing, he got a sudden, strong whiff of cigarette smoke. Smoke from that yellow cigarette, he was sure of it!

Fishing out his pocket notebook and reporter's pencil, Trey made a quick note of the carriage and room number and then hurried on towards the dining car and the inevitable lecture from his father about punctuality, reliability and tardiness...

3 THE ELEGANT LADY

It was at lunchtime the next day, somewhere in between Milan and Venice, that Trey saw Monsieur Mustache again. The man, who was sitting at a table in the dining car when he and his father came in, had his back to them, but Trey knew exactly who it was: no one else on the train had hair *that* shiny. And now he also knew his name.

Trey had not wasted his morning. This time, when his father had hauled a sheaf of papers out of his attaché case and uncapped his fountain pen, he hadn't sighed and rolled his eyes because this gave him the excuse he'd been looking for to leave his father to whatever work he just *had* to do and go investigating.

There had been a *Ne Pas Déranger* sign on what he thought was Monsieur Mustache's room when he'd gone past and Trey hadn't found him anywhere else on the train, which had meant that there wasn't much else he could do except go back to his own cabin and read, or watch the Italian countryside go by out of the window. It was as he disconsolately made his way towards his own carriage, dragging his feet, that he spotted the box of matches on the ground.

He stopped and lifted the nearby ashtray cover. Inside were a couple of yellow cigarette butts which, from the smell, had quite recently been stubbed out. Deduction? Why that Monsieur Mustache had not long ago been out for a smoke!

Trey bent down, picked up the matchbox and examined it; the glossy black cover with gold lettering advertised something called *La Plume Indigo Cabaret* and closer inspection revealed that, while it sounded full, it in fact contained only spent matches. Another deduction: Monsieur Mustache was a somewhat tidy man. And the find gave Trey an idea.

He set off and eventually found a door with a small

black and white enamel sign on it which read *Bureau de Steward* – the Steward's Office. Trey knocked on the door, aware that Trent Gripp would probably just have walked in; it opened to reveal the office to be more of a cubbyhole, really, in which a tiny desk, a chair and the steward himself just about all fitted. Acting as innocent and honest as he possibly could, he handed in the "lost property", which he said he *believed* belonged to the man back in Room 6, the one with the grey hat.

"That's right, isn't it, Monsieur?" Trey asked, smiling his most open and sincere smile.

"*Numéro six?*" the steward replied, arching one eyebrow; then, making a face like he'd smelled an old sock, he glanced from the matchbox in Trey's hand to the list on the wall behind him. "You must mean Monsieur Giovedi..."

"That's him," beamed Trey, holding out the matchbox. "Will you give this back to him – I would've, but it said 'Do not derange' on his door, and I didn't want to make him mad..."

"When I next see him." The steward nodded curtly, taking the object from Trey's hand as if it was quite possibly infectious.

* * *

So "Monsieur Mustache" turned out to be called Monsieur Giovedi, which Trey thought sounded as if he maybe came from somewhere like Italy, which meant that he was more than likely called Signor Giovedi. But the real surprise, as he and his father came into the dining car, was that Signor Giovedi had a travelling companion. And she was a platinum blonde looker, in the style of that actress Thelma Todd, right off the cover of one of his magazines!

His father didn't seem to notice as he was in mid-flow, telling Trey about all the things they were going to be doing during their three-day stay in Venice. And, as Trey had figured, it boiled down to yet more museums and galleries, but so far there had been no mention of theatres, which was what his mother would call "a small blessing".

The head waiter beckoned them down the carriage and then pulled a chair out from the table he'd chosen for them; Trey's father ushered him forward, and as he went past Signor Giovedi and his companion he realized the woman was wearing the exact same perfume his mother liked to use. This really did *not* fit with the way she looked – because she looked absolutely *nothing* like his mother, who was undoubtedly very pretty, but would never make the cover of *Black Ace* in a million years.

The seat that Trey was shown to gave him no view at

all of the Giovedis (he was assuming they were married – although he knew that any sleuth wishing to stay alive till the end of a story should *never* assume anything and always worked on the facts alone – as he hadn't thought to check the woman's left hand as he went past).

"Close your mouth, Trey, you look like a galumph... and whoever it is you're staring at, stop."

Trey snapped back, automatically sitting up straight and looking at his father. "Just daydreaming, Pops... wondering what was for lunch."

"Well *I'd* recommend looking at the menu, rather than anywhere else..." Putting on his horn-rimmed reading glasses, T. Drummond MacIntyre II picked his menu up and followed his own advice, nodding to himself as he turned over the pages. "All very nice..."

A cursory glance told Trey that, in his father's own words, he begged to differ. For a start the menu was all in Italian and just looked so darned *classy* that it was obvious there wouldn't be anything on it he'd like. "I suggest you have the *Fettuccine alle polpette*, Trey, followed by the *Gelato alla fragola*," he said as the waiter came and stood by their table. "That should keep you going until we reach the hotel."

"But Pops!" Trey watched the waiter's pencil hover over his pad. "Can't I just have a baloney sandwich, please?"

"My suggestion is that you have something very like your beloved spaghetti and meatballs, Trey, followed by strawberry ice cream."

Trey looked up from the menu to find his father smiling back at him. "You do?"

"Sure. But if all you want is a sandwich, I'm sure I can ask the waiter here to see what they can rustle up for you..."

"Spaghetti and meatballs, right?"

Trey's father nodded.

"Okay..."

4 ONE STORY ENDS...

After a very satisfactory lunch, try as he might, Trey had been unable to get away from his father to continue his investigations on the train, and, now here they were, with their luggage, chugging off towards the Hotel Excelsior on some overcrowded water taxi.

"...they call this a *vaporetto*, son," came the answer to an unasked question, "because it's steam-powered."

Frankly, as far as Trey was concerned, they could call the boat whatever they darn well liked, because he was not happy. Not happy at his failure to come up with the goods on the mystery couple, *or* that the chances of him *ever* finding out whether he'd been on to anything or not had vanished into thin air.

The last time Trey had seen Signor Giovedi (and the woman who might, or might not be Signora Giovedi) was when he'd caught a glimpse of them on the platform after the Orient Express had arrived in Venice at the Santa Lucia train station. In all the chaos which had accompanied their exit from the train, and the subsequent turmoil caused by their transfer to the *vaporetto*, Trey found it completely impossible to keep track of the dark grey fedora, and so the story of The Man With the Pencil Mustache stuttered to a somewhat disappointing conclusion. Unless, of course, he saw them again...

As Trey had disconsolately traipsed after his father, following him through the station hall, the chance sighting of a freshly stubbed-out yellow cigarette butt had given him a moment's hope that he was going to be able to pick up the trail, but it was not to be. The Giovedis had gone.

Standing on the wooden deck of the small steamer, Trey held on to the brass rail, aware that his feelings of disappointment were fading as he stared around him... at least the latest stage in his summer journey looked like it was getting off to a good start, if the view from the boat was anything to go by. Whatever bones he had to pick with his father about his definition of "not working" (and there were so many of them they would make up an *entire* chicken's carcass, in his opinion) Trey had to admit that, despite all the telegrams and such, he had certainly seen some sights on the trip so far. And here he was staring at another one: the city of Venice.

All the stuff he'd read in the guidebook that his father had handed over the moment he'd asked a question ("Look it up for yourself, son...it's the best way to learn") hadn't done anything to prepare him for the real thing – *a whole city built on the water!* Unfortunately, *not* on actual stilts, as he'd first imagined. The place was incredibly old, and looked like something out of a storybook where pirates and swashbucklers were to be found – *and* it had canals for streets!

Everywhere Trey looked there were people going this way and that in small boats the guidebook had said were called gondolas. The stories he was going to be able to spin when he got back to Chicago! The gang at school were just *not* going to believe what he'd have to tell; he wished he'd tried that bit harder to get his father to buy him a camera so he could prove what he'd seen as he knew that Morty, Will, Stan and Ronnie would be spending the summer at their families' South Shore houses.

It turned out that their hotel was not in the actual main part of Venice, but on a long, thin island some way off it, in a place which Trey's father said was called the Lido ("...you get the best views and don't have to deal with the hoi polloi, son...") and it looked to Trey very much like he was going to be stuck away from whatever action there might be in yet *another* smart and stuffy joint. No doubt the kind of place where nothing less than the very best behaviour would be the order of the day. Every day.

The hotel looked like a palace, with uniformed flunkies everywhere, and crystal glass candelabra, velvet curtains, fancy gold decorations, marble floors, walls, stairs *and* statues; it had huge ornately framed mirrors and dark, impenetrable oil paintings on the walls, with acres of polished brass and wood as far as the eye could see. He was, Trey thought, staying in a museum with sea views. Once again, not his personal idea of a holiday.

Their accommodation turned out to be a very large suite, which certainly had the kind of scenery you might admire, if you liked palms and seascapes, like his dad. There might be more interesting places around and about, but how to get to check them out? The answer came moments later when a troupe of maids arrived to unpack their cases, which he had a good idea might well cause a major distraction.

"Pops?" he asked as his father, who spoke no Italian, began trying to tell the maids where things were to go.

"Yes? What?"

"Can I go for a walk?"

"Sure, sure..." His father glanced over his shoulder, then returned to the job in hand. "No, *not* in there..."

At which point Trey made a hasty exit and set off to see what, if anything, there might be for him to do.

It was while he was wandering across a big terrace that he spotted something that looked worth investigating. A large group of people (as he got closer he saw that there seemed to be a lot of women among them) was surrounding three men in uniform, and hanging on their every word. As they were speaking Italian, Trey had no idea why this was. Nevertheless he circled the group, as this was by far the most interesting thing that was occurring, but it wasn't until he'd got a bit closer, and got a better look at the three men, that he realized they were flyers.

One of the men made some comment and gestured rather grandly behind him, over the parapet and in the direction of the sea, and everyone clapped and cheered. Trey went over to have a look at what the man had been pointing to and found himself staring at the most beautiful sight in the world – if you liked planes, that is – because, floating in the pale blue, mirror-flat water, moored to a pier, was a bright red racing seaplane. And if Trey knew his planes (which he liked to think he did, having his own scrapbook of photos and stories clipped from newspapers and magazines) he was sure that what he couldn't drag his eyes away from was nothing less than a Macchi M.52 – just about the cat's pyjamas when it came to aeroplanes!

"Oh boy…" he whispered. "What a beauty!"

"You like the planes?"

Trey spun round to find one of the flyers standing next to him. *"Like* them?" he sputtered. "I *love* them – I was lucky enough to see Mr. Charles Lindbergh's ticker-tape parade in New York, you know!"

"I think you are quite a lucky boy, then," the man smiled. "Did you meet him?"

"Me? No sir, I was thirty-three floors up in a skyscraper."

"Well right here, not even three *metres* away, is Major Mario de Bernardi, the man who won the Schneider Trophy race in your country last year – and I believe is going to win it once again *this* year. Would you like to meet him?"

"Who, me? *Yes, sir!*"

* * *

As Trey lay in bed, stomach full to bursting after a blow-out of a meal (he had actually lost count of the number of courses he'd eaten), his head was reeling from the sights and sounds of what had turned out to be possibly the very *best* day of his life. Not only had he met a record-breaking flyer – one of the fastest men on Earth – he'd actually been allowed to sit in his plane! The very same streamlined machine that would be taking part in the Schneider Trophy speed contest, which he'd discovered was happening *right here in Venice* in a few weeks' time! Boy, would he love to be there!

But, Trey thought as he began to nod off, there was a fat chance of *that* ever happening. When your father was one of the MacIntyres of MacIntyre, MacIntyre & Moscowitz ("One of the busiest engineering concerns in the whole of the continental US, son...right up there near the top of the heap!"), business always came first and always, if at all possible, ran to a tight schedule. Which was why this sudden change of plan to take a trip on the Orient-Express had made him wonder...what on earth could his father be up to? The schedule and plan had been strangely abandoned.

5 THE DAY TRIP

The next day things really did *not* go according to plan. At least not to the plan that Trey had worked out in his head (but failed to discuss with his father), which was a long list of all the terrific ways he could spend his time. These mainly boiled down to staying as close as he could to the Italian flyers, with the general idea being that, while he knew there was no space for him actually in the single-seater Macchi racer, they might have *other* planes and he *might* get to go up in one of them. You just never knew.

And as it turned out, Trey never did discover, because his father had other ideas entirely for what he and his son were going to do with their time. True to form, his father would not hear of *any* changes to the schedule he had planned. Especially, he explained, as he had lately been feeling a tad guilty about the amount of calls he'd had to deal with and cables he'd had to reply to and send. He told Trey he'd put aside the entire day for them to "do" Venice together.

T. Drummond MacIntyre II, as was his way, had got it all meticulously worked out (something he had failed to discuss with his son), so Trey found himself being taken out to a *vaporetto* – a private one his father had hired for the day – which was going to take them on a tour of the Grand Canal, and more. As well as the boat, his father had also hired a guide for the day, Signorina Aurelia Sanpietro, who had the disadvantage, from Trey's point of view, of being neither young nor pretty (she was no picture, as he had no doubt his mother would have put it); she also had a somewhat loud, not to say operatic voice and spoke English with such a heavy accent that Trey found what she said made no sense at all. The word "formidable" had immediately sprung to his mind when he'd been introduced to her.

As the three of them left the hotel he saw the bright

red Macchi M.52 bobbing at its mooring, and his heart sank. Mechanics were fussing about under the engine cowling and he could see someone – it looked like Major de Bernardi – pulling on a flying cap and generally getting ready to go. It would be just his luck if it turned out he was flying off for good, or at least until the race in September. The Italian flyers were the most exciting thing in this place.

Trey hung back, watching the last-minute preparations, imagining what it would be like if *he* was over there lending a hand…imagining that he *was* there and that he'd spotted something, like a leaking fuel line – which, if he *hadn't* been there, would have gone unnoticed and led to a fatal crash! He saw himself being congratulated for foiling the sabotage plot (with the honour of nations at stake in this race, it just *had* to be sabotage) and given his own leather flying helmet and goggles in appreciation…

"Trey! Trey, will you stop daydreaming – the boat's here and we're ready to go!"

His father's voice dragged Trey unwillingly back to reality just as he was about to accept a celebratory glass of champagne and the scenario disappeared like a burst bubble.

"Coming…" he mumbled, with one last glance over his shoulder at the plane, then traipsed off towards the pier where his father was standing, hands on hips, waiting for him.

Once they were on their way his father explained to Trey exactly what the day held in store for them. And, entirely no surprises, it turned out they were on their way to see a long list of churches (which it would, apparently, be a crime not to see), galleries that *must* be visited, piazzas it'd be a shame not to sit in and bridges that had to be sailed under and walked over. Oh joy. An *entire* day of Culture, with one very big capital "C".

Trey had done his best. He really had. He hadn't huffed and puffed too much, in his opinion, and while he hadn't actually said a lot he hadn't complained either, but by mid-afternoon he was truly beginning to lose the will to live. He just knew that if he saw another *Palazzo*, *Campo*, *Piazza* or *Ponte* he was going to get a twitch in one of his eyes and start to gibber quietly to himself, but then things took an interesting turn: he got lost.

And there was no way round it, the situation was entirely his fault. One moment he'd been following his father, who was following Signorina Aurelia Sanpietro (an endlessly enthusiastic mine of information about her beloved city), and the next he was on his own in the middle of some enormous open space.

Well, not *actually* on his own as wherever he now found himself was jam-packed with visitors...hundreds and hundreds of them. Quite possibly *thousands*, Trey thought as he stopped and stared around, vainly trying to spot his father and their jabbering guide.

The buildings flanking the sides of the huge square were colonnaded and intricately decorated, bedecked in flags and covered in all kinds of coloured marble. The one he was facing, which he could see towering over the heads of the crowds surrounding him, looked like something out of an Arabian Nights tale; with its cupolas-on-top-of-other-cupolas roof and the statues and mosaics all over the front, it was, Trey thought, more like an enthusiastically over-decorated cake than a building.

Pushing his way through the crush of people he searched with an increasing desperation for his father (what *had* he been wearing this morning? He hadn't really been paying attention...), with one ear cocked for the sound of his name being called (surely, by now, his disappearance had been noticed...hadn't it?) and the other listening for Signorina Aurelia's telltale bellow.

But there was no sign of his father, and if anyone was calling for him it was lost, as was Aurelia's voice, in the rising babble and chatter from all the other tourists. Trey looked back the way he'd come, then realized that he couldn't work out which way that might actually have been, and even if he did know it wouldn't do him any good because he didn't know where he was.

It slowly dawned on him that not only did he not know his present location, where he'd been, or how to get back to where the boat had docked, he also hadn't the *slightest* idea where they were going to visit next. And to top it all, although he'd heard any number of people speaking English wherever they'd been so far, right now he didn't understand *any* of the languages he could hear all around him.

This sense of being alone, abandoned and cast adrift made him feel really strange. In fact, Trey suddenly realized, if he didn't get a good grip on himself he might possibly... No! That was *not* going to happen – T. Drummond MacIntyre III was *not* going to panic! He was going to find his own way back to the hotel, which might be a bit of a problem because that would entail a boat ride and he had no money. But as his grandfather, the original T. Drummond, had always said, where there was a will there was a way. And if Gramps said it, it had to be true.

Trey knew beyond a doubt that he had the will (he was a go-getter, everyone said so) it was just that he was more than a little unsure of what the way was. Venice, as he knew from the map back at the hotel, was a random maze, completely unlike Chicago and New York, which had been built on downright sensible grid systems. Weaving through the milling crowds he might, for all he could tell, be going round and round in circles; as that thought came to him, he himself came to a circular break in the crowd, at the centre of which stood a lady who was either being attacked by hordes of pigeons or was in some way orchestrating them.

Rooted to the spot, Trey watched the seething pool of speckled grey birds, the woman carelessly waving her arms and laughing as the birds flew up and around her in a fluttering, feathered cloud. He was so transfixed by the sight that he forgot, for a moment, that he was lost and alone...then the hopelessness of his situation returned, and like a wave crashing onto a beach it washed away his moment of happiness, leaving him feeling desolate.

Straightening himself up, Trey took a deep breath: this was *not* the way a private eye would act! Doing something – anything, really – would be far better than moping around and doing nothing. He was sure he could find some boat to take him back to the Excelsior (the place was full of them), so all he had to do was work out how to pay for his ride. It was as he was wondering how he could successfully mime "I have money back at my hotel!" that he got the distinct impression, like at the train station in Paris, that he was being watched.

The boy, older than him, was wearing a threadbare, faded red shirt, baggy sailcloth trousers and leather sandals; he was sallow-skinned, with a dark, wispy smudge on his upper lip and badly pockmarked skin, and he was staring right at him through narrowed eyes. This time, unlike in Paris, Trey knew in his gut that he hadn't got the wrong end of the stick, especially when the boy didn't look away the moment he'd been noticed, instead making it obvious he didn't care that he'd been caught out. A half smile, half sneer curled the boy's lip as he glanced to his left and nodded to someone else. A signal, Trey realized, that it was time for the someone else to make their move.

Heart in his mouth, Trey searched the crowds for the person the boy might have been signalling to, at the same time trying to move away and lose himself in the forest of people. He'd been targeted. They thought he looked like an easy mark (he'd show them!) and they were going to rob him, or worse, once they discovered he had no money – and for all he knew there were enough of them to already have every escape route sewn up tight. On top of which he did not have a whole heap of options open to him. He could stand his ground and fight, hoping that someone would step in and help him, or he could run.

Trey caught the glint of polished, sharpened steel in the boy's hand, and he ran.

Head down and heart thumping he dived into the crowds and pushed blindly past whoever was in his way, aware that this was *not* winning him any friends, but in no mood to care. He wanted to look behind him to see if he was being followed, but he was too worried that there might be someone in front of him that he really needed to avoid. Then, out of the corner of his eye, to his right, he saw a flash of red and realized the boy with the knife had somehow manage to snake his way through the crush and was closing in on him like a fox on a chicken.

Trey veered left, wondering if now was the time *he* should begin squawking "*HELP!*" at the top of his voice, and then found that he'd broken clear of the crowds (which, although they'd slowed him down, had also provided some protection) and was now out in the open. A snap to catch. Spotting a narrow street that kind of looked *vaguely* familiar, Trey pelted for it, cursing the fact that getting his penknife out of his pocket *and* running as fast as he could over these ancient and very uneven flagstones was just not possible.

He was fast, but his pursuers were faster, hungrier, more desperate…and, as it turned out, there were three of them, and they knew their way round Venice a whole lot better than he did. Trey had figured he'd at least two people right on his tail, but he had no idea there would be a third waiting for him halfway down the almost passage-like street he'd run into.

He was trapped!

Skidding to a halt the moment he saw the third figure barring his way, Trey glanced over his shoulder to see Red Shirt and his friend sauntering towards him. No need to run now that their quarry had nowhere to go. And then there he was, surrounded, with Red Shirt right in front of him, a thin, humourless smile drawn across his face; up close Trey could see that the boy's teeth were bad, his clothes worn, his hands dirty and fingernails bitten. He was just some street-poor kid, like the ones back home in Chicago, from round Maxwell Street and Addams, parts of town he knew only by reputation. But before Trey could start to feel sorry for the boy he jabbed a finger hard in his chest.

"*Dammi tuoi i soldi.*" The boy rubbed two fingers against a thumb. "*Dollari, ragazzo – ora!*"

The boy wanted money, that much was obvious, and he was demanding it – with menace – which Trey did not appreciate one bit. He jabbed back.

"Beat it, palooka!"

Silence, as a slightly confused look passed across Red Shirt's face...and then, as the boy sneered, the silence was broken by a metallic *TCH-KK!* and Trey found himself going cross-eyed as he stared at the needle-sharp point of a switchblade. He had, in his anger, forgotten about the knife.

"*Cretino...*"

Trent Gripp would not have stood for this kind of treatment, but like he always said, there were times when acting brave was the height of foolishness, and to his mind this was beginning to look like one of them. The trouble was, having already acted the hard-boiled tough guy, no matter what he did now he was going to be in deep trouble because when this joker started to cut up rough, things were going to get bloody. And the blood was going to be his...

"E'scuse me, you have trouble, kid?"

Trey whirled round without thinking and was amazed to see a man in a dark suit and grey fedora, standing a few feet away with both hands in his trouser pockets...a man with a heavy accent, a pencil mustache and smoking a yellow cigarette. Signor Giovedi! Before he had a moment to say anything, like "Watch out – he's got a knife!", Trey saw Signor Giovedi slowly unbutton his double-breasted suit jacket and let it swing open to reveal...the butt of a pistol.

"*Lasciatelo anddre, ragazzi.*" Signor Giovedi jerked his thumb for Red Shirt and his friends to leave, and be quick about it.

"Perché, che dice?"

"Why? *Ho una pistola – va bene?"*

Trey felt like a pawn in a very dangerous game of chess, stuck in the middle of the board and unable to move because there was a knife still hovering far too close to his face for comfort.

"I thin' you should be ready to move, my small fren'."

"Me?" Trey hated the fact that his voice had sounded like a mouse's squeak.

Signor Giovedi didn't answer, instead he took his right hand out of his suit pocket and let go a fistful of copper and silver coins. They went everywhere, bouncing off the ground like metal rain, flashing as they spun like miniature tops. The sudden gesture, the noise, the fact that this man had thrown away *money* as if it was rubbish, distracted Red Shirt and his friends long enough for Signor Giovedi to grab Trey's arm, hauling him away and back out into the *piazza*.

Trey was lost for words as he stared at Signor Giovedi, taking a moment to realize that his beautiful companion was standing next to him. She was observing him with an unnerving *Mona Lisa* smile on her face (although he had to say the rest of her looked nothing like the picture his father had dragged him to the Louvre in Paris to see). What on *earth* was going on? Had he been right all along and this man really had been following him and his father...and if so, why take such a risk, even if he had got a gun (and exactly *why* did he have a gun?). Questions tumbled around his head, unable to find a way out of his mouth.

"You hunky-dory now?" Signor Giovedi lit a cigarette.

"You ask me, this kid is the picture of lost, César."

The possible Signora Giovedi was chewing gum and spoke with a raw Brooklyn accent, pronouncing the name as Say-zar; she did not, Trey thought, talk anything like the way she looked, but after what he'd been through *any* American accent was posi-lutely fine by him.

"You lost, kid?" she queried. "Not that I'm surprised in a place like this...they got streets here narrower than a Mexican gunslinger's tie, right, César?"

César nodded. "E'zactly, *amore mio*...narrow streets. Where you got to be, *amico*? Where you stay?"

"The Excelsior."

"Very chi-chi." The woman raised one finely-plucked eyebrow.

"*Molto*," agreed César. "Less go, *ragazzo*, we take you there..."

Trey hung back, torn between having no idea what to do and really wanting to be taken back to the hotel. Any of the private eyes in *Black Ace* would, no doubt about it, trust their instincts...but those instincts would also be backed up by the fact that those PIs were packing heat, just like Signor Giovedi was. And what kind of person wandered round on *holiday* with a gun in a shoulder holster?

"You coming or what, kid?" the woman asked, blowing a large, bright pink bubble.

Quite why the sight convinced Trey it would be okay to go with them he didn't know, but it did.

Which was how, after being treated to a large vanilla ice cream, covered in *real* milk chocolate shavings, and an orange fizzy drink, Trey found himself in a water taxi, being delivered back to the Hotel Excelsior by César and Isabella Giovedi – as unlikely a pair of rescuers as it was possible to imagine.

César was in business (and although he never specified the business of what, Trey thought he had a pretty good idea that it was probably as legit as a nine dollar note), and Izzy, as she like to be called, offered that she had been in the business of show, as she put it, before the two of them had met and married. César did say that he came from Naples, and he was taking his wife on a grand European tour, explaining in great detail that although Izzy was also Italian she had been born in New York. But he never said one word about what Trey thought of as The Incident, and neither did he explain how come they'd just *happened* to be there or why he'd stepped in to help. While Trey was desperate to ask, he thought that maybe it would be better if he just accepted what had taken place and left it at that; frankly, he was *so* glad to still be in one piece that he was prepared to believe whatever he was told.

César and Izzy had waltzed into the Excelsior and taken him right up to the manager's office, where César explained about Trey getting lost and he and his wife finding him; he did not, to Trey's great relief, go in to too much detail. The manager, acting as if this sort of thing was a daily occurrence, replied that he would make sure every effort was made to contact Mr. MacIntyre and inform him of his son's safe return. All the while Trey stood in the middle of the proceedings feeling like he had to be asleep and dreaming as it was all so *weird*.

After saying a loud and quite embarrassing *Arriverderci!* – Izzy planting a kiss on *both* his cheeks – Trey went up to the suite to wait for his father. Who, if Trey was any judge, was not going to be best pleased with how the day had turned out. Once he'd washed off

Izzy's lipstick he went out onto the balcony; the red Macchi M.52 had gone, as he'd feared it would have, and a boat was now moored where it had been when he'd left the hotel in the morning.

It had been a strange day – a *lot* more exciting than he'd ever imagined it would be – plus, in the process of getting lost and being found, the story of The Man With the Pencil Mustache had gotten even *more* mysterious. He didn't want to believe his rescuers had been lying to him, but wasn't it really a bit too much of a coincidence that they should be right there when he needed them? If that kind of thing ever happened in one of his stories he always thought the writer was taking the easy way out and not being very original. There was now no doubt in his mind that there was *definitely* more to this than met the eye. But exactly what was completely beyond him.

6 "WHERE EAST MEETS WEST, SON!"

The next day Trey's punishment for getting himself lost turned out to be going back with The Formidable Aurelia to every *single* one of the places he'd missed seeing the previous day. All on his own, while his father stayed at the hotel. No doubt working.

He was beginning to wonder why on earth his pop had ever brought him on this trip if all he was going to do was act like he was in the office *all* the time; while none of his friends ever spent *that* much time with their fathers, except Morty Sorgenson, because Mr. Sorgenson was a lot older and had retired, he had thought that, being as how they were on holiday, it might have been different. It would be nice to get to know each other better, like he felt he knew his gramps. But then he did spend a lot of time with Gramps – or, more correctly, his gramps found the time to spend a lot of time with him. Trey often spent some of his holidays on the ranch Gramps had outside Topeka.

Trey's trip turned out to be more torture than punishment as he spent the whole, entire day being bludgeoned at high-volume with a continuous barrage of "information of interest to the touristic person", followed by questions to see that he'd been paying attention.

It seemed to Trey as if Signorina Sanpietro hardly paused for breath from the moment they left the hotel until she delivered him to the station at 15.30 precisely, where his father was waiting to get back on board the Orient Express. Next major stop Belgrade, capital city of the Kingdom of the Serbs, Croats and Slovenes, which Trey thought had to be the longest name for a country *ever*, and with the added attraction of being somewhere The Formidable Aurelia wasn't.

Thankfully the stop was too short and too late in the day to actually do anything remotely cultural, but long enough for Trey's father to send a telegram back to the

Chicago office and give him a lecture about the city and its environs ("Belgrade lies on the Danube, son – which is, at over 1,700 miles from start to finish, Europe's second longest river") and for him to write his mother a postcard. Then, according to Trey's pocket compass – the one that had been in his other jacket the day before, when he'd really needed it – the train began to travel in a more south-easterly direction as it made its way towards the Bulgarian capital of Sofia.

The fact that this happened to be one of the oldest cities in Europe was somewhat less fascinating to Trey than that it was also his mother's name, except she spelled it Sophia. On the other hand, the news that the country's Tsar, Boris III, had escaped assassination not once but *twice* in the last couple of years – and that the Tsar's actual name was Boris Klemens Robert Maria Pius Ludwig Stanislaus Xaver Saxe-Coburg Gotha – was the kind of information that you *could* call enlightening and well worth knowing.

It was, though, a pretty dull journey as his father had made it quite clear that he must not, under any circumstances, bother anyone. Which meant that he was banned from investigating who and what was on the train (you never knew, the Giovedis might be on board...). People, his father pointed out, did not want the company of an over-imaginative boy. Trey did not believe this was true, but the veto had been imposed and he could tell by the look on his father's face that it was not about to be lifted any time soon...

It was at seven o'clock in the morning, two boring days after they'd left Venice, when the train finally pulled into Constantinople's Sirkeci Terminal. The station was on the western side of the city ("...where the Orient casts its eye at Europe across the straits of the Bosphorus, son!"). It all sounded mighty romantic, as his gramps would put it, but the reality came as something of a shock.

Stations were – by the very nature of their being full of trains, luggage and people attempting to get themselves somewhere or other in a hurry – very noisy, dirty and somewhat chaotic places. This one was chaotic, dusty and *very* hot, but, Trey had to admit, it was also pretty grand, with what looked like a fancy restaurant and a lobby that was the size of a small church.

But once they were finally on their way to the hotel – there had been something of a scene at the station when it looked like a piece of their luggage might have gone missing – it became clear to father and son that *everywhere* in Constantinople was generally a heck of a lot noisier and hugely more chaotic than the station had been. And not as grand, it had to be said.

The taxi which their porter had hired for them was a dusty old Studebaker *"Big Six"* that had, much like its unshaven, fly-blown driver, definitely seen better days. The canvas of the landau top was ripped, crudely mended and full of holes which Trey thought looked like they'd been made by bullets; it would, his father commented, be about as useful as a colander if the weather should decide to turn rainy.

And the rest of the car was not in much better shape: the leather seats were split, spilling out coarse stuffing; what wood veneer was left in the car had lost its varnish; and the yellowing windscreen was sporting a couple of large cracks. Parts of the car were actually being held together by string and the whole contraption gave every impression that it would fall apart if the driver attempted to go faster than a slow trot – luckily something the crowded streets were never going to allow to happen. But at least it was a car. Most of the traffic on the streets seemed to be either horse-drawn or pulled by a mangy donkey.

The Hotel Pera Palas, which was where people who had travelled down to Constantinople on the Orient Express stayed, was some way from the station and getting there turned out to be more of an adventure than a mere taxi ride. The driver, who shouted, swore and spat his way through the traffic, finally negotiated them onto the Galata Bridge, which Trey knew, from his cursory perusal of his father's guidebook, was going to take them across a stretch of water called the Golden Horn.

Because he knew this was a somewhat legendary and historic geographical feature Trey readied himself for yet another of his father's lecturettes, but it failed to arrive, a fact Trey put down to the disconcerted, not to say stunned expression on his father's face; he really did not much like spitting, or shouting, for that matter. Left to his own devices Trey was free to stare out at life in Constantinople.

This did *not* look like a place that was big on the kind of culture he'd recently been subjected to, which was fine by him, and the journey across the low, wide, slatted wooden bridge, while unbelievably slow because of all the pedestrians, was fascinating. People were fishing off the sides, and everywhere he looked there were sail boats of all sizes, steamboats and tiny skiffs zipping about like water bugs on a pond.

As out of control as the city appeared to be, the Hotel Pera Palas was the total opposite, an atmosphere of dignified calm descending on them as they made their way through its glass-canopied double doors and up the marble staircase to the lobby, followed by their luggage.

The aura of tranquillity lasted as long as it took for Trey's father to discover that they *should* have taken the hotel's gratis limousine service from the station, and steered well clear of the cab rank the porter had been well tipped for taking them to.

Once in their suite, with staff bustling round unpacking, delivering messages, mail and refreshments and generally bringing a sense of order back into his life, T. Drummond II finally allowed himself to relax. Sitting, his legs stretched out, in a large armchair, with a fresh whisky and soda in one hand and a cork-tipped Craven A cigarette in the other, he suddenly sat upright, as if pulled by a string.

"Did I tell you, Trey?"

Trey, a pistachio-and-honey concoction in his mouth and something similar in his hand waiting to join it, shrugged in an "About what?" kind of way; his mind was completely elsewhere as he had *never* tasted *anything* like these pastries before and they knocked doughnuts and Danishes into a cocked hat, in his opinion.

"It's all organized!"

Trey swallowed. "What is, Pop?"

"Remember I mentioned it, in London? About the Stanhope-Leighs?"

The second pastry stopped halfway to Trey's open mouth. "The Stanhope-Leighs?"

"The Trade Secretary at the British embassy here in Constantinople? That cousin of my friend Templeton... you, my boy, have a head like sieve," he said, shaking his own. "He has children about your age, Stanhope-Leigh, that is, and, while I am otherwise engaged, as I will have to be for more than a few hours most days, I asked him if you could spend some time with them. There was a message waiting for me here to say that it's all been organized..."

7 EVERY CLOUD...

Trey was lost for words as everything about the Stanhope-Leighs came back to him in all its dreadful detail...there was a boy, Arthur, and – worse – a girl called Christina, and they had a tutor or a nanny or somesuch, and they would, according to his father, all be the best of friends!

As if.

Back in London Trey had not really paid too much attention to what his father had told him; Constantinople had seemed so very exotic and far away that in his mind it had not even ranked as a faint possibility that he might eventually meet – *and have to spend time with!* – these kids. And now the chickens were coming home to roost, or whatever the saying was his gramps liked to use, and it was about to happen.

"But…"

"No 'buts', Trey, we have already discussed this, I explained it all to you and you agreed that it would be fine." A hotel flunkey knocked and came into the room carrying a small silver tray with an envelope on it which he presented to Trey's father, who fished a tip out of his waistcoat pocket, swapping it for the letter. "And like I said, once I finish all the business I have to do here," he waved the envelope as if to underline quite how busy he was, "it'll be just you and me, I promise."

Knowing there was absolutely no point in him arguing, Trey left his father slitting open the envelope with a letter opener, went to his room and unpacked his stash of magazines. At least when he was between the covers of an issue of *Black Ace* or *Dime Detective* he could pretend none of this was happening – that he would never even so much as have to *bump into* this kid called Arthur, or his sister.

Picking up an issue he let himself imagine what it would be like to be a real-life gumshoe with a baffling case to solve…like what exactly did his father do all day? He had to admit that he didn't have much of a clue what his father's business actually involved, mainly because he wasn't there to watch and his father didn't really talk about it much. But then again, was it really a subject worth investigating? Somehow, he doubted it.

That night they had dinner at the hotel; it was very grand, in a stuffed shirt kind of way: all balustrades, polished marble, gleaming brass, wood and silver. There were, it seemed, pieces of cutlery for *every* dish that arrived (of which there were many). It took Trey a few minutes to realize that his father was in a mood and that it wasn't, as far as he could tell, anything to do with him. From experience he knew that there were two courses of action he could take: act as if there was nothing wrong, which would mean a meal spent mostly in silence, or ask what the matter was and see what would happen. At home this might mean being frowned at for being nosey, but here in public, in the middle of a smart restaurant, Trey was willing to bet that he had a chance of getting away with it.

"You okay, Pops?"

T. Drummond II glanced up from discreetly spooning soup (he was never one to slurp, even in private) and raised his eyebrows quizzically. "I think so, why?"

"I don't know…you seem concerned." Trey had heard his mother say this under similar circumstances to some effect, and figured it could work for him.

"No…no, I'm fine."

"Oh, good…" Trey stared at the swirling patterns his spoon was making in the soup; this was not working quite the way he'd hoped and he didn't have a Plan B.

"Although there is *one* thing I've been meaning to tell you…"

Trey looked up suddenly, his spoon hand jerking and sending a small, mainly green wave onto the pristine white of the starched cotton tablecloth.

"Trey!"

"Sorry, Pops…" Trey surreptitiously moved his side plate to cover as much of the spill as he could. "What were you going to tell me?"

"I was *going* to say that the plan has had to be changed slightly…just for tomorrow."

"Oh?" Trey sat up even straighter than he had been.

"That letter, the one which was delivered soon after we arrived?"

"Yes?"

"It was from a Miss Jane Renyard, the tutor who looks after the Stanhope-Leigh children." Trey's father put his spoon down in the finished position and dabbed his mouth with the corner of his napkin. "Apparently there has been a mix-up – I won't bore you with the details – but suffice to say that she, Miss Renyard, cannot take you tomorrow. I hope you won't be too bored trailing around after me all day."

"Me? No!"

"Best behaviour, Trey; at all times. I am going to have to leave you waiting in outer offices and such and I don't want to come back and find you've been causing trouble."

"Who, me?"

"Yes, you, my boy." Trey's father did smile at this point. "You surely haven't forgotten Fifth Avenue, have you? I know I haven't."

Trey checked the soup out again as the memory of a scene he'd tried hard to forget ran through his mind... how could he have known that tipping back a chair would lead to such chaos? That when the chair fell backwards it would shoot him across the floor – in a kind of reverse somersault – and straight into a table with some fancy Chinese vase on it? There was no way! He could still see the look on the secretary's face as she stared at him, surrounded by shards of pottery, her mouth open like a fish in a bowl.

"It won't happen again."

"Promise?"

"Cross my heart and hope to die, Pop; this time

I'll take a magazine so I won't get bored."

For the rest of the meal Trey felt like a condemned man who had been given a reprieve, even if it was only for twenty-four hours; still and all, another day without having to deal with some snotty English boy and his Dumb Dora of a sister was something to be celebrated, which he did by having two desserts and managing to persuade his father to go for a stroll around the streets near the hotel before he went to bed.

The night was warm, and the air full of a heady perfume (gardenias, according to his father); he figured that this place was what the word "exotic" had been invented to describe...the buildings, the people, the clothes they wore, the activity (boys rushing here and there with brass coffee trays that hung down from decorated handles, spilling nothing) and men sitting outside cafés puffing away at complicated glass contraptions, three feet tall and with thin hosepipes attached to them. His father said they were called hubble-bubbles, but to Trey they looked like science experiments.

It was as they were passing by a bustling café that he noticed something very odd. Three men, dressed in regular suits, not the flowing robes that most people seemed to wear, and all with impressive mustaches, were sitting together at an outside table, smoking cigarettes and drinking tiny cups of coffee; when one of them caught sight of Trey and his father, he did a double-take and then swiftly turned his back on them and whispered something to his neighbour.

Trey glanced up at his dad to see if he had noticed the event but saw that he was looking in the exact opposite direction; glancing back Trey saw all three men staring at them, and simultaneously try to appear as if they were doing no such thing. It should have been a comic moment, like in a Buster Keaton movie, except there was definitely a sinister feel, especially when one of the men got up and hurried inside the café. The last thing Trey saw the man do was pick up the earpiece of the telephone on the wall and jiggle the lever to get an operator.

Who, he wondered as he and his father turned a corner, was that man in such a hurry to tell about seeing them? It was like the guy had recognized them, or at least recognized his father, which he supposed was possible, if he'd been to Chicago. But why all the whispers and secrecy? What was *that* all about?

8 SPOTTED!

Trey had pondered long and hard about telling his father what he'd seen, but in the end thought better of it. If he did, all that would happen was that his father would probably blame "all that rubbish" he read for "disturbing his imagination", and then proceed to confiscate his magazines; it would not be the first time.

So he kept quiet, but decided to keep his eyes peeled for any signs that they were being observed, followed, or in any other way spied upon; he would also take his notebook and pencil and record everything he saw, just in case. Even though he thought his father should be happy, as this would give him something to do with his time, he hid the notebook inside one of his magazines so the fact he was making observations would remain a secret.

It turned out his father had got the hotel to organize a car and driver for the length of their stay and they emerged from the hotel after breakfast the next morning to find a gleaming, red car (and an equally smart chauffeur, who actually spoke a bit of English and, as it turned out, didn't spit either) waiting for them outside. This was the first non-American automobile that Trey had ever seen and when they arrived at his father's first appointment, even though he knew he should go with his father and see if he could glean any information about what he was doing in Constantinople, he instead elected to stay outside with the car and have a good look at it.

"Any trouble *at all* and you are grounded, young man – back to the hotel and in your room for the rest of the day!" T. Drummond II turned to the driver. "Make sure he's here when I get back...there'll be no tip if he isn't."

"Understand, *effendi*." The driver shot a glance at Trey. "He will be here."

Trey watched his father walk away, making for the front entrance of an office building, in the large foyer of which he could just make out the nameplates of all the companies that had offices there. He frowned, wondering if he'd made the wrong decision.

"You trouble, boy?" the driver enquired, breaking into Trey's thoughts.

"Me?"

The driver nodded.

"Not if I can help it, but sometimes it seems like no matter what I do I can't avoid it, you know?"

The driver nodded again. "I know." He pointed at himself and made a serious face. "Four boys," he said, and then his face broke into a grin. "Four times trouble!"

"What kind of automobile is this, mister?"

"This," the driver smiled proudly, patting the dashboard, "is Citroën 10 HP Type B12! Very perfect!"

Five minutes later the driver, whose name Trey had found out was Ahmet, had the hood of the car up and was showing off the engine, which looked tiny compared to the cars at home. Trey was, however, impressed by how *clean* and *polished* everything was; it looked like you could eat your dinner off the engine block.

"Three gear," Ahmet held up three fingers, "*seventy-five* kilometre the hour! *Very* perfect!" Ahmet did a thumbs up and grinned at Trey.

Hauling out his notebook, which had a handy list of conversions on the back page (should you wish to know there were four poles to a chain, and that one kilometre was 0.62 of a mile) Trey calculated that 75 k.p.h. was actually just over 46 m.p.h. Not bad, he supposed.

He was chewing on the end of his pencil, trying to remember exactly how fast he'd been in his father's Chrysler Imperial, when, across the street, he saw someone staring at him, a face he recognized. For a moment he thought he'd spotted Signor Giovedi, from the train, but then he recognized the mustache and realized it was the man from the café the previous night – the one who'd rushed off to make a phone call!

The moment the man realized Trey had seen him he turned away and hurriedly walked off down the street, losing himself in the crowds. Stunned by what he'd seen, Trey didn't know what to do; if he chased after the man he would, one, probably not find him, two, probably get lost himself, three, definitely get grounded and, four, guarantee to lose Ahmet his tip. His father was nothing if not a man of his word.

The facts were plain: something was definitely up, but all *he* could do was stay where he was and remain on high alert; which was nothing like a real detective... *nobody* told Trent Gripp what to do. Then he remembered his plan and turned to the first page of his notebook, checked the time on the Ingersoll his parents had given him for his last birthday and wrote it down:

9.23 a.m.

"What's this street called, Ahmet?"

"This?" Trey nodded. "This *Tarlabasi Bulvari*."

Trey noted the name, although he spelled it *Tallabassy Bullvary*, and then jotted down:

Spotted man from last night (outside café, near hotel) watching the car. And me.

He wrote as neatly as he could, at the same time trying to remember what the man looked like, but had to admit to himself that he looked a lot like a lot of other people he could see walking by. In the end he noted:

Grey suit, mustache, black hair (slick, kind of like Gramps does it with Macassar oil). His eyebrows join up. Untrustworthy?

Trey closed the notebook and, as he put it and the pencil back in his jacket pocket, saw Ahmet looking at him questioningly. "I think we're being followed," he said, relieved to be telling someone what he thought was happening. Even if Ahmet didn't believe any of what he said he wouldn't tell him he'd been reading too many detective magazines.

"Now?" Ahmet slowly looked left and right.

"No, they went."

"You sure?"

Trey nodded. "Pretty much."

"We keep eye to the grindstone, you and me. Okeedokey?"

"Sure, that'd be nifty."

"Lot of following in this city." Ahmet nodded, mouth downturned and one eyebrow raised. "Lot of secrets."

"Yeah, what kind?"

"If *I* knew, young mister, they wouldn't be secrets, yes?" Ahmet grinned, showing a fine set of tobacco-stained teeth. "Very much of the spy here, and all that they do."

"*We* don't have any secrets, Ahmet...my dad's just a businessman and all *he* does is a *lot* of deals, no secret about that." Trey shrugged. "I don't know what the deals are, but I'll bet they're nothing worth getting excited about."

"Secret is thing someone *think* they don't know." Ahmet raised both eyebrows this time. "And think *must* be found out..."

9 EYES IN THE BACK OF HIS HEAD

The rest of the day, except for a break for lunch at some swanky French restaurant where Ahmet sat outside in the car waiting for them, followed much the same pattern: his father would give Ahmet an address, he'd drive there and Trey would wait in the car while whatever business there was to do was done.

A perfect arrangement, to Trey's way of thinking. He didn't have to go up to some stuffy office (where he'd have to be on his very best ever behaviour, *all* the time), and could carry on conducting his counter-spying activities without any interference from his father – who assumed that the close interest his son and heir seemed to be taking in his environs, as they drove around the city, was in some way educational.

And in a way it was. Trey learned about religion (there were an *awful* lot of mosques in Constantinople), history (Ahmet was proud to have been a soldier in the Great War, prouder still to have fought, and beaten, the English at the momentous Battle of Gallipoli), and of course, cars (Ahmet was also a fount of knowledge about all things to do with automobiles).

While all this random knowledge came his way, Trey attempted to see if they were being followed, which he found was an extraordinarily tough job in a city as frantic and buzzing as Constantinople. How could you possibly tell, in the pandemonium of traffic, animals and people, who was tailing whom? It was incredibly frustrating, and the pages of his notebook became filled with crossings out, half-finished sentences and no definite sightings at all.

It was as his father strode off for what he promised was his last meeting of the day (at 4.47, as recorded in his notebook) that everything changed.

"You see it?" Ahmet asked without turning round.

"What?"

"Do not make big fuss...be gentle with your look."

"Where, Ahmet? *Where* do I look gently?"

"Behind, on other side of street. Black car."

Trey took his time, first looking completely the other way (to confuse anyone who might be watching him) and then risking a quick glance where Ahmet had said. All the cars on the other side of the street, and there weren't *that* many of them, were black. He immediately looked away. "Which..."

"Ford, Model T...very dirt and scruff."

Trey shot a swift peek over his shoulder. "Ah, *that* black car...what about it?"

"It follow."

"You sure?"

"Very sure."

"Can you see who's in the car – is there a man in a grey suit?"

"I think possible. And other one."

Trey sunk down in his seat and wondered what on earth to do next as he hadn't actually worked out what to do *if* he was right. He went over in his head what he knew: firstly, that the man in the grey suit probably suspected he'd been spotted outside the very first office they'd visited (otherwise why disappear so fast?); and secondly, that as the man hadn't seen him leave the car with his father, presumably he knew he was still in it. Hunched down, Trey knew he'd feel a whole lot more confident with a snub-nosed gat tucked into his shoulder holster, like a real PI.

It was right then that it occurred to Trey that *he* had no reason to hide...that it was The Man in the Grey Suit (another great title for a story, which he scribbled down) who was the one who didn't want to be seen. Remembering the advice of numerous of his favourite detectives he realized that the best thing he could do was act normal and confident, as if he had no idea anything was happening – what the hero in one of the stories he'd read recently had referred to as "lulling 'em into a false sense of security". And then there was one other thing a good shamus should do – he should make a note of the car's licence plate for future reference.

"Ahmet – can you see what the number on that car is from where you are?"

Trey watched as Ahmet adjusted the rear-view mirror, and then shook his head. "It hide behind another car."

There was, then, only one thing for it: he had to get a better view and memorize the number, because he could hardly stand there taking notes. Which meant getting out of the car and walking across the street. What could possibly go wrong? Only that his father might catch him disobeying his instructions to stay where he was, but, as their next stop was the hotel and there was precious little left of the day to be grounded in, Trey thought that the risk was worth taking.

Except he didn't want to get Ahmet into any kind of trouble; that would not be fair.

Trey looked across the street and saw what looked like a stationer's and he had an idea. Pressing his pencil hard onto the page he bust the lead. "Would you look at what happened?" He held up the broken pencil. "Could you come with me over the road, Ahmet, 'cause I need to go to that shop and get a sharpener?"

"Bad idea, I should say so." Ahmet shook his head as he opened his door. "I go, I come back, you stay, is better one."

Before Trey had a chance to say anything to Ahmet about why he *really* wanted to go to the shop, Ahmet was the other side of the street and the next moment had disappeared through the shop's door; Trey glanced nervously at the building his father had gone into, half expecting to see him come striding out and get an extra knot in his tie because his driver wasn't where he was supposed to be. If there was one thing he knew his father hated it was being kept waiting.

"I make note, through window."

Trey jerked round to find Ahmet getting back into the driving seat. "You did *what*?"

Ahmet looked over his shoulder, smiling as he held

up his right hand, a folded slip of paper gripped between the two fingers. "You want number of car, no?"

"You are the best!" Trey reached over and took it.

"But can't make note in book without this."

Trey looked up and saw that a brand-new pencil had appeared between Ahmet's fingers.

After copying down The Man in the Grey Suit's car licence plate, Trey found absolutely nothing else to put in his notebook on the drive back to the hotel; with his father lost in his paperwork he was free to observe all he liked, and with the late afternoon traffic slowing their pace down to a crawl it was a perfect situation for careful observation. But, as hard as he looked (trying his best to make it look as if he *wasn't* looking hard) he even lost sight of the one car he knew had been following them.

Glancing at his father, sitting next to him making occasional notes on the papers he was reading, Trey found it hard to believe he could possibly be involved in anything that might make him the kind of person who got tailed. But he had been a bit distracted recently, so could he be tied up in some shady deal or other? Surely not…and then it occurred to him that, from what he'd seen today, they must appear to be very, *very* rich indeed; back home he'd never really thought about how they lived, or how much money they had. So could this all be leading up to a robbery? The thought gave him the jitters.

Trey sat back, frustrated and vexed that, though he was *sure* something really was up, he had no evidence whatsoever. And evidence, as any gumshoe worth his pay cheque knew, was everything. So a day which had started with so much promise ended on a rather flat note as Ahmet pulled their car up in front of the hotel and a doorman rushed to assist in his father's exit. Trey realized that that was it – tomorrow would be *entirely* different – no chance for any sleuthing. He got out, aware that his father was organizing for Ahmet to pick him up first and deliver him to the Stanhope-Leighs. He slouched into the lobby, the truly awful prospect of what was in store for him the very next day hanging like a thundercloud over him...

10 FROM BAD TO WORSE

Trey stood in front of the house and looked from the imposing brass door knocker to the polished bell-pull, not knowing which one to use...not actually *wanting* to use either and wishing he was still in the back of the car that Ahmet had just driven off in to go and pick up his father. In the end he didn't have to choose as the double doors swung open on well-oiled hinges to reveal a smartly dressed older man in a black suit, starched shirt, wing collar and neat black bow tie standing in the gap, looking down his nose at him. These people had a *butler*?

"May I be of assistance?"

"I'm T. Drummond MacIntyre III."

"Ah, just so…you've come to play with the children." The butler stood back and indicated that Trey should enter the house. "Do come in, sir, and I will go and fetch their governess, Miss Renyard."

Play? With the *children*? Trey, momentarily lost for words, watched the man, whom he now noticed was wearing white gloves, walk away. What kind of nightmare had his father cooked up for him? Visions of spinning tops, dolls, construction sets and even *sand pits* flashed before his eyes. He looked over his shoulder, just in case, by some miracle, Ahmet had come back to rescue him, but the wide, cobbled street was silent and empty. Absolutely no sign of anyone following him.

When he looked round he saw a woman with close-cropped dark brown hair and wearing a blue sailor-style dress coming down the hall towards him, smiling broadly. Just exactly what, he wondered as she approached, did she have to be so happy about?

"Young Master MacIntyre! How *nice* to meet you…*do* come with me and I'll take you up to the playroom and introduce you to Arthur and Christina, who can't *wait* to make your acquaintance!"

For one blissful moment Trey thought he *had* to be dreaming, *that at any moment* he'd wake up in his bed, back in his room at the Pera Palas, and none of this would be happening...but then he was walking down the hallway, Miss Renyard's trilling voice bouncing off the silk-lined walls as he dragged his unwilling feet up two flights of stairs (were these kids locked away in the attic?), and not one word of what she was saying sinking in.

"...and after we have been to the archaeological museum, and had a *lovely* picnic lunch in the park, we shall take a little look at the Topkapi Palace, which I have heard is quite..."

The fact that this torture was going to happen to him until his father's work was done was beginning to really get to him, and the thought occurred to him that maybe he could fake some kind of terminal illness and get to stay at the hotel instead; he wouldn't even mind if they took him to the hospital.

"...only been with the family a week or so, but the children are *very* nice and I'm *sure* you'll all get along swimmingly togeth..."

Or maybe, *maybe*, he could have an accident! Nothing *too* serious, just bad enough to mean he couldn't go off on any trips to yet *more* museums and palaces, as he really did think, apart from not wanting to spend any time at all with these Limey kids, he had been to more than enough since leaving Chicago.

"…and here we are!"

Trey stumbled to a halt to see Miss Renyard had stopped walking down the wide corridor and was standing by a door. She was smiling at him again, in that way he'd noticed some adults did when they really *wanted* everything to be all right, but had an inkling that this might not necessarily be the case.

"Shall we go in?"

"Okay…" Trey nodded, and then remembered his manners. "Thank you."

"What a *sweet* accent!" Miss Renyard chirped as she opened the door and beckoned for him to follow her. "Arthur, Christina – here's your new friend!"

Trey was still trying to work out what this Miss Renyard had meant by him having an *accent* – when it was as plain as the nose on a pug dog's face (as his gramps would say) that *she* was the one who sounded funny – as he entered the room. The *play*room, he reminded himself. And indeed there was the girl kneeling on the floor surrounded by a whole gang of dolls – all dressed much like she was, in frills – and the boy, standing at a table covered with an electric train set, the engine clickety-clacking its way round the extensive track.

"Children!" Miss Renyard clapped her hands. "This is – what *does* the 'T' stand for?"

"Trey," Trey replied.

"Trey…what an *unusual* name."

"Not really." Arthur Stanhope-Leigh let out a bored sigh as he expertly slowed the train down to take it through a sharp bend in the track. "He's called T. Drummond MacIntyre the *third*, isn't he…and 'trey' sort of means three, so it's obvious, really."

Trey did not appreciate being talked about almost as if he was an object, and one that wasn't even in the room, and felt like boxing this stuck-up kid's ears to show him just *how* much he didn't appreciate it.

"Well *I* think it's a very nice name."

Trey saw the girl had got up from the floor and he noticed for the first time that, with her mass of blonde, curly hair and big, blue eyes, she was actually quite pretty. If you liked that sort of thing. Which he wasn't sure he did.

"I'm Christina." She came over, holding out her hand, which etiquette demanded Trey shake. "And that's my absolute *pill* of a brother whom you should really just ignore. He wants to be the Prime Minister when he grows up," Christina added, as if that explained everything. And then she finally let go of Trey's hand.

"Well, now that we've all met I think it's time to think about going!" Miss Renyard nodded and smiled, somehow managing to look relieved and anxious at the

78

same time. "I'll go and make sure Cook has everything ready and then tell Stevens to meet us with the car at the front of the house. I'll send Molly up to get you..."

Trey watched her go, wondering how many people this family had working for them.

"What do *you* want to be when you grow up, MacIntyre?"

"You talking to me?" Trey frowned at Arthur, who hadn't even bothered to look up as he spoke.

"I do believe I must have been, old chap."

Trey took a deep breath, aware that Christina was watching him like a hawk and for some reason he did not want to come out of this looking like he'd been gotten the better of. "Let's make a deal, okay? You keep out of *my* hair and I'll keep out of *yours*. That way I won't have to boot your keister, *old chap*."

Christina snorted with laughter, Arthur's ears turned a deep puce and Trey could tell that the next few days were not going to be a cakewalk, by any manner of means. On top of which, every moment he had to put up with the Stanhope-Leighs was a moment he was unable to spend with Ahmet, watching his father's back (as he knew all the best shamuses called checking to see if someone was being followed). The thought of what he might be missing made Trey grind his teeth.

11 THE VISITOR

Ahmet closed the car door, and as he went back to the driver's seat Trey heard Christina call out.

"Bye-eee! See you tomorrow!"

He also thought he could hear Miss Renyard urging Arthur to say goodbye as well (some hope *she* had); he sank back into the seat, giving a desultory wave as Ahmet drove off, and then going cross-eyed at the thought that what he had just been through was going to be repeated, *ad nauseam*, for some days to come.

"You have good day?"

"No, Ahmet, I do *not* have good day...how about you?"

"I fine, thanking you."

The two of them sat in a reasonably easy silence for the next few minutes as Ahmet guided the car through the traffic; the last thing Trey wanted to do was go over what he'd done that day, and he was exhausted from the strain of answering the seemingly continuous stream of questions from both Miss Renyard and Christina about what it was like to live Chicago. Not to mention constantly having to stop himself from biffing that sneering worm Arthur, who seemed a real sneaky type. Which reminded him...

"Did you see anyone following you today, Ahmet?"

"Were back again."

"They were?" Trey snapped upright.

"Yes, that men, from day before today. Different car, but I spot all the same; they follow like lost puppy."

"Are they here now?" Trey whirled round and looked out of the rear window, amazed with himself for not having thought to check before.

Ahmet shook his head. "Not *you* they like to see. Only *Mr.* Macktire."

"What happened?"

"Not so much. I just see the car, and two men with it, here." Ahmet reached up and tapped his rear-view mirror.

"Where's my father now?"

"I took him Pera Palas – in the room, maybe?"

"And the people who've been on your tail all day, you think they're still there outside?"

Ahmet shrugged eloquently. "I not magic...can't not see from here."

Trey couldn't tell if Ahmet was joking with him or not, but he was more concerned with the fact that, while he'd been traipsed around yet another collection of cultural artefacts, in the real world a story his father was blissfully unaware of was still unfolding – *and he should have been involved!* And the more Trey thought about it the more it was like the novelette he'd read recently; in *The Nearly Man*, a hapless detective had always been one frustrating step behind the man he was trying to catch, and he now knew *just* how he felt...

"You tell Mr. Macktire?" Ahmet asked, interrupting Trey's thoughts.

"You think I should?"

Ahmet did another of his meaningful shrugs.

"He more than likely wouldn't believe me, if I did." Trey shrugged to himself. "But what if something happens to him if I *don't* tell him?"

They were stopped in traffic and Ahmet raised both hands off the wheel and looked up at the roof as he shook them, like he was offering a heartfelt prayer. "*What* to do, eh? *What* to do?"

Standing in the lift as it cranked its way up to the seventh floor, Trey was still unsure of what would be the best course of action. Experience ("The cheapest form of education available!", as his gramps, who seemed to have a saying for almost every single occasion, would put it) had taught him that his father would be disinclined to believe *him* if he said there was somebody following him, so maybe he'd believe someone else. Someone like Ahmet. But then again, maybe not, and he did not want to get Ahmet into any kind of trouble with his father.

He watched the operator bring the lift to a halt at his floor and pull the two sets of doors to one side so he could exit; walking out he turned right to go to their suite. Maybe, if his father had had a good day, and seemed to be in an amenable mood, he could try and work the conversation round to what he *might* do *if* it so happened he *was* being followed. Just to get his father at least thinking about the idea. Trey was still deep in thought, planning how the conversation might go, when he reached the door to the suite...and found that it was ajar.

If Trey had owned hackles they would have been standing right up on end. As it was, even though it was hot, he felt a shiver run from the nape of his neck to the base of his spine. What could this mean? The only way to find if it was "nothing" or "something" was to go in. So Trey gently pushed the door open just enough so that he could get his head through the gap, and then peered in.

So far it was "nothing", an empty lobby area leading into the sitting room, which was also, as far as he could tell, empty. And then he heard voices coming from the room his father was using as a study. His father must have a visitor. So now there was only one thing for it: he had to actually go in. Taking a deep breath he pushed the door open a little bit further and slipped into the lobby.

He knew that, under normal circumstances, he would have marched in and, as he was always being told, really made his presence felt. But these circumstances were not, he reckoned, quite normal. So, like any gumshoe worth his salt, he quietly made his way into the sitting room ("Keep *schtum* and keep breathing" was, as he was well aware, every private eye's watchword), stopping by one of the leather chesterfields and listening.

He could still hear the voices – a low, loud rumble from behind the closed study door – but not what was being said; and then, out of the blue, the burning question of what his next move should be was answered by his father bellowing "GET OUT!" and what sounded like a fist being slammed onto a desktop. Trey ducked down out of sight behind the leather sofa.

Later, when he reran what had happened, he supposed he'd hidden because he'd felt like he was about to be caught red-handed eavesdropping, but at the time, with the study door slamming open, it seemed like the only thing to do and the right place to be.

"I've just about had it up to *here* with this!"

Trey had never heard his father get in such a lather, even after the unfortunate incident involving him and a rather ugly piece of porcelain – a family heirloom, no less – in which the statuette had come out distinctly the worse for wear.

"I told you, Mr. Paklov – *I do not know WHAT you are talking about!*"

"We shall see," the man said in a heavy accent.

Behind the chesterfield, his heart in his mouth, Trey found that he could see everything that was happening reflected in the glass panels of a corner cabinet opposite him; worryingly, he realized, that meant he could also be seen. But, thankfully, his father and the unwelcome guest were too busy yelling at each other to notice.

"Get out, *now*, or I'll have you thrown out!"

"You will regret…"

As the man turned to leave the suite, without finishing his threat, Trey caught a fleeting glimpse of him jabbing an accusing finger. He was a stocky, balding individual with steel-rimmed glasses and dressed in a creased suit which, as he swung round, flapped open to reveal a brown leather shoulder holster. Complete with gun…

In the silence which followed first the slamming of the suite's door, and then the study's, Trey sat on the floor behind the sofa, stunned. What was a man – *with a gun!* – doing arguing with his father? What he'd just witnessed was like a scene straight out of one of *Black Ace*'s novelettes, although they didn't regularly feature people hiding behind chesterfields wondering what to do next.

Trey started to get up, then sat down again. A little voice was telling him that to make an appearance too soon would be a bad move (how would he explain his sudden appearance to his father?); so he stared at his watch, waiting as the seconds ticked by and built up into what he considered to be enough minutes so that he could *arrive* home and not have seen or heard anything he shouldn't have.

Luckily, his father stayed in his study so Trey was able to tiptoe back out into the corridor, turn right around, take a deep breath and come straight back in again (doing his own bit of door-slamming) as if nothing untoward had happened. On the outside he tried to look the way he imagined he should after spending the day with the likes of Arthur Stanhope-Leigh, while on the inside he nervously waited to put his foot in it and say the wrong thing.

He needn't have worried as his father's mind was plainly elsewhere and dinner that evening was a pretty silent affair, which ordinarily Trey would have tried to do something about. But, as it meant that he didn't have to recount every last detail of his loathsome day, this time he let it go and spent the time trying to think about what he'd seen from behind the chesterfield. He really needed to talk everything through with someone, but the only person who would understand was Ahmet. And so, while part of him was dreading the next day, the rest could hardly wait.

12 THE OTHER SIDE OF THE COIN

"Could you park up for a minute, Ahmet? I *really* need to have a talk with you."

"Surely can do." Ahmet abruptly swerved left across the road in front of a horse-drawn cart piled high with bales of cloth, jamming on the brakes and screeching to a halt; turning round he looked expectantly over the seat at Trey, who felt like a shuttlecock in a badminton match. "Yes? What you say?"

"Right..." Trey rearranged himself, got out the notes he'd written before turning his bedside light out and proceeded to tell Ahmet about what had happened when he'd got back to the suite the day before, describing everything in as much detail as he could. Especially the gun.

"This is quite odd."

"And how! Did you see a balding man with those kind of metal-rimmed glasses yesterday?" Ahmet shook his head. "Well, keep an eye out for him today, okay? It sounded like he had unfinished business with my father."

"I keep *both* eye out for him, you should not worry!"

"My pop called the guy 'Mr. Paklov'...that's a Russian name, right?"

Ahmet made a half-nod, half-shrug, as if what Trey had said was *probably* true.

"There a lot of Russians in Constantinople?"

"I think a lot of *everyone*, all looking at each other from over the top of newspapers..." Ahmet mimed the scene he was describing, his eyes swivelling left and right. "Like a game..."

Trey found it difficult to get what had happened out of his head – who was this mysterious (and armed) Mr. Paklov, and what had he been accusing his father of? It was a real stumper and he didn't see how he was going to be able to find *any* answers, as he could hardly question his father about what had happened, and was now being driven away from the scene of the crime. Sometimes, in his opinion, life was less than fair.

But, despite himself, Trey had quite enjoyed the day. Because Christina was off spending time with a friend, Miss Renyard had taken him and Arthur first to the Naval Museum and then, after lunch, across town to the Military Museum; here, amongst so much else, they'd seen the famous Janissary Band perform, resplendent in red and gold uniforms with swords stuck into their sashes.

After a day spent closely examining guns and ships, cannon and swords, an uneasy truce came into existence between the two boys, and while it could not be said that they were in any way *friends*, they had got along well enough to make them really quite late in getting back to the house. Ahmet was waiting to pick Trey up, and by the time they shook hands at the front door, watched by a beaming Miss Renyard, for whom this event was a major triumph, their mutual disrespect had lessened somewhat.

"Well?" enquired Trey the moment he was inside the car.

"Excuse?"

"Did anything happen? Did you *see* anyone, like the bald guy in the glasses? Were you followed?"

"Yes."

"Yes?"

"Yes." Ahmet started the car, shifted into first and drove away.

"What d'you *mean*, Ahmet?"

"All of it happen."

Trey almost took a bite out of the seat in front of him he was so frustrated. "So tell me *what* happened, Ahmet...like *I* told *you* this morning about what went on last night..."

"There was not so much excitement."

"I don't care."

"You *don't* want me to say now?"

"Pull over will you, Ahmet? I'm going to come sit up front and we are going to sort this out..."

He had, *finally*, managed to get the whole story out of Ahmet, who was right about it not being very exciting, although it *was* quite worrying. A car *had* followed them – a different one from the day before – and Ahmet *had* spotted a person trying too hard not to be noticed (who pretty much fitted the description of the balding, gun-toting gentleman Trey had seen storming out of his father's study), but that was about it.

By the time they got back to the Pera Palas they were considerably behind schedule, which Trey was sure would not go down all that well; except, if he got in first with how terrifically he was now getting on with Arthur Stanhope-Leigh, and described in detail all the things they'd done. That might do the trick.

"Okeedokey, Ahmet..." Trey slammed the car door shut, hoping that his father would be in a better mood at dinner as he wouldn't mind a meal that wasn't spent mainly in silence. "See you tomorrow morning, thanks for the ride."

Walking into the hotel lobby, Trey stopped for a moment as the seriousness of the situation hit him: whatever his father's mood tonight, there were no two ways about it, he was going to have to bite the bullet and tell him about the people following him. His father was too much at risk to keep it a secret any longer.

Five minutes later he was standing outside his suite, staring at the door, which, once again, was ajar. His mouth drier than a whole packet of cheese crackers, Trey poked his head through the gap and listened.

Nothing.

It was only as he strained to hear if the suite really was as quiet as it seemed to be that he noticed the chair. He could see the back of it, tipped over and lying on the carpet...and then he thought he could see what looked like broken glass. For a moment Trey almost turned and rushed back to the lift to get help, but a vivid picture of his father, collapsed on the floor, flashed in his mind's eye and he knew that what he should do was go in and ring down to reception for help.

He pushed the door open and ran into the sitting room...which was empty. Empty, in that his father wasn't there, collapsed on the floor and in dire need of assistance, although it was full of all the signs of a very hasty and untidy exit indeed.

"Pops?"

Trey's call got no response and a sense of dread slowly crawled over him as he attempted to figure out what had occurred; and then, standing alone in the middle of the room he suddenly became aware that he could hear something, but had no idea what it was. A little voice in his head told him that he'd never find out if he didn't shake a leg and go and take a look, and a swift tour of the suite provided him with four facts:

1. The noise was the phone in the study, off its hook.
2. His father was nowhere in the suite.
3. This was not a robbery as he'd found his father's money clip by his bed.
4. There was what looked very much like blood on the study carpet.

So, he thought, sitting down on the edge of the chesterfield, the money clip still clutched in his hands, it looked like there had been "an incident"...his eyes wandered round the room, taking in exactly what kind of a state it was in...an incident during which someone had gotten hurt bad enough for there to have been some blood spilled; whose, he did not know, or want to think about, because *his father was missing*!

This appalling thought was echoing round his brain when he heard people talking, outside in the corridor, before he remembered that he hadn't closed the door behind him when he'd rushed in. It took precious seconds for him to realize that he couldn't understand a word of what the people were saying, and a second or two more before he recognized one of the voices. As he heard the door being pushed open, it hit him – it was the bald man (the bald man *with the gun!*) from the night before. Like a March hare he leaped up and without thinking ran for the nearest bedroom – his father's – some ancient survival reflex kicking him into action so he didn't simply sit and wait to be caught. What his next move was going to be he hadn't really worked out, but there had to be *something* he could do.

If this was New York, and he was Trent Gripp, he'd no doubt have been out the window, down the zigzag fire escape and on the street before you could say "Black Ace". But this was him, in Constantinople, and he had no idea if there was a fire escape to make for.

Closing the door behind him as quietly as he could his eyes darted round the room. He could, he thought as he stuffed the money clip in his jacket pocket, hide inside one of the massive wardrobes, although they'd have to be pretty stupid not to find him there. Or, if he pulled one of the chairs over, he might just be able to get up on *top* of a wardrobe before the men came to look in the room...but then the chair would be way too much of a giveaway.

Trey was just considering the possibilities offered by getting right under his father's massive double bed when he saw the door. Or rather, *another* door. The bedroom had a *second* door! Which, if he was right, led out directly into the corridor...he ran across, heart in mouth...to find it was locked! He stopped breathing. Then he noticed the key was in the lock, just below the handle, and let out a huge sigh.

In the other room he could hear growled conversation, doors slamming and the sound of something delicate breaking. He had seconds before one of the men came into the bedroom...he turned the key...which stuck. He broke out into a sweat, gripped and turned as hard as he could until the mechanism, stiff from underuse, creaked and finally unlocked. Trey took a deep breath and opened the door. If the man with the gun had left someone outside in the corridor he was done for, but one swift look was enough to tell him that the coast was clear, and as he was about to close the door behind him he had what he thought was a pretty neat idea. Reaching back he took the key and locked the door from the outside, and as he did so he was sure he heard someone come into the bedroom. Just made it!

Running back down towards the suite's main door he reached into his trouser pocket and brought out his own key to the suite. The one he'd taken with him in the morning, in case his father was still out when he got back from the Stanhope-Leighs'. As he ran he heard the unmistakeable sound of a door being rattled as someone tried to open it; he speeded up, skidding to a halt in front of the double doors, which were still slightly open. As the rattling turned to hefty thumping, accompanied by loud shouting, he heard another voice coming his way. Trey yanked the door shut, inserted the key and twisted it to the right; the well-oiled deadbolt slid into place seconds before whoever was on the other side grabbed the handle.

Just made it, again.

Streaking off down the corridor, pleased, and not a little amazed that the plan had worked, Trey did wonder quite how much longer his luck could hold.

The question was answered moments later by the crack and splinter of a shoulder, or possibly a foot, being put through one of the doors and a heavily accented voice bellowing *"STOP THIEF!"* after him.

Trey almost did stop in his tracks he was so shocked. Thief? Him?

The racket was obviously having the desired effect as up ahead he saw a door to another suite open, a quizzical face appearing round it.

"STOP HIM!"

Without waiting to see if this person would do as he was being asked, Trey sped past him and, instead of carrying on towards the elevators and stairs, rounded a corner and took the first available turning. Where it went he had no idea, but at least he figured he'd be out of sight.

Out of sight, and trapped in a dead end.

The narrow service corridor went nowhere, ending in a curtained window. Horrified, Trey was just about to make as swift an exit as possible, back the way he'd come (by now sure he'd blown *any* chance he'd ever had of finding an actual escape route) when he saw what, for all he knew, was a cupboard, but desperation made him carry on; reaching the door he flung it open and was relieved to see not a storeroom full of sheets and soap, but a staircase. It wasn't as luxuriously appointed as the one the guests used, having bare walls and no carpet, but it went down, and that, thought Trey, was all that counted.

His feelings of relief lasted a total of about two and a half flights, which was when he heard the clatter of footsteps – which unfortunately did not in any way sound like those of a maid – coming after him.

With four more floors to go Trey knew he didn't have a cat's chance of getting out of the hotel before he was caught and…well, he didn't know what these men would do to, or with, him but what he did know was that he had no desire to find out. It was as he went from leaping three steps to five steps at a time that he noticed the chute cover set into the stairwell wall. It was like the ones in their duplex apartment back home in Chicago. Into which garbage was flung, and down which it hurtled, direct to the basement.

Trey slid to a halt by the next chute he came to and pulled the bottom-hinged cover open, half expecting the rank odour of leftovers to assault his nostrils. It didn't, and breathing a sigh of relief he hauled himself up and into the dark, vertical shaft, which he figured must be used by the staff to send sheets and stuff to the laundry. The chute's cover, which was weighted, shut behind him with a soft clunk…

13 WHERE TO NOW?

Wedged in the laundry chute, which had sides not much wider than his shoulders, Trey waited, listening for the sound of his pursuer going past. He didn't have to wait for long, and soon all he could hear was the dull echo of the man's stampeding footsteps coming back up the shaft.

He was so relieved that he let out a deep breath and allowed himself to relax for the first time since he'd heard the men outside his suite. This had the unfortunate side-effect of making him lose his grip in the chute and he'd plummeted a good ten, twelve feet before he managed to stop himself. Now he was twelve feet from the way he'd gotten in (and had hoped to get out), and more than likely the same distance from the chute entrance on the next floor. This situation was bad enough in itself, but then he heard footsteps coming back *up* the stairs, stopping on the floor below.

Trey looked down between his legs...what was going on? Four floors below he could see the pale, grey square that had to be the end of the chute; it was a long, long way away. Then light spilled into the shaft as someone opened the cover one floor down and poked their head in, checking up and down the chute. Trey froze. This was it, the chase was over and he was about to get caught!

But maybe not...at least not yet.

Below him the man swore and slammed the cover shut, his footsteps disappearing back down the service staircase. Once again Trey let out a sigh of relief, but this time he didn't relax; he realized he hadn't been caught because, suspended *above* the man in the pitch black of the laundry chute, he'd been invisible!

All he had to do now was shimmy down to the next floor, maybe the one below, get out of the chute and go find the Manager's Office. He would *surely* be safe there, and the Manager could call the police or the

Embassy and do all that official stuff – in fact, it now occurred to him, whatever had happened to his dad might have *nothing* to do with those men turning up... his dad might've had a minor accident or something and gone to hospital. It was possible. And if *that* was the case (you had to look on the bright side) the Manager would know all about it. But then, as he cautiously edged his way down the shaft, Trey had a worrying thought: if his father have been kidnapped from their suite – *in broad daylight, no less!* – maybe the Manager might *not*, in fact, be the best person to go to. He could be in on the whole thing, or being bribed or blackmailed or...or not. Trey wouldn't know until it was too late.

As Trey slid past the third-floor chute entrance, it crossed his mind that if this *was* all an inside job, it would likely be someone below the Manager – like in the detective stories set in English country houses where it was the butler who'd always done it. Or like the yarn he'd read called *The Inside Out Job*, where the bank's security guard had been in on the heist. Deep in thought, and assuming that the two men chasing him had gone elsewhere to look, Trey wasn't trying to be particularly quiet so he was quite unprepared when the chute door he'd just gone past opened and a hand reached in to grab him by the arm.

"Got you, boy!" exclaimed a gruff voice, of the kind

that Trey knew for sure belonged to a gun-carrying type.

Everything then seemed to happen all at once.

Trey lost his grip and fell, except the hand holding his arm kept a tight grip and he found himself dangling in mid-air; but, as he felt himself being inexorably pulled back up, a bundle of sheets and pillowcases came tumbling down the chute and enveloped him, and however much of his captor was poking into the shaft. As the two of them struggled to untangle themselves, Trey felt the man lose his grip.

It was a couple of seconds before he fully took in that this sensation of freedom was *also* what it felt like to plunge, uncontrollably, towards the basement. However far down *that* was...

As he dropped like a stone, Trey was acutely aware that he could well be just moments away from becoming strawberry Jell-O. Fading into the distance above him he could hear shouting, but the only thing that concerned him now was what was going to happen below. It was as he thought that he probably wouldn't *ever* get to see his parents again (and that he'd yet to send his mother a postcard from Constantinople, like he'd promised he'd do at regular intervals and from everywhere they visited) that he landed with a muffled thud which knocked the breath out of him.

Gasping for air, and batting various piece of dirty washing out of the way, Trey attempted to stand up. This was not as easy as it might have been. The loose mound of laundry, piled in the huge wicker container that had caught him, acted much like quicksand, so that the more he tried to get out, the further down he seemed to go. When he finally surfaced he found himself, the arm of a pair of striped pyjama tops draped over his head, staring at a very confused and startled maid, unused to seeing guests come down the laundry chute.

"How do I get out of here – I mean the hotel, not..." Trey flipped the pyjama arm off his head and pointed down at where he was standing, "...*this* place?"

The maid frowned, in a way that made it perfectly clear she didn't speak a word of English.

"Okay..." Trey clambered over the side of what he now saw was basically a massive laundry basket on wheels, jumped to the floor and brushed himself down. He thought for a moment, then mimed going up to a door, opening it, checking no one was there and then tiptoeing through. "Out," he said, "so no one sees me, right?"

The maid looked none the wiser.

"Okay, how's about this..." Trey mimed a grand arrival. "*Front* entrance." He pointed to himself and shook his head; then he did a "tiny door" and the tiptoe thing and pointed to himself again, nodding and grinning. "*Back* entrance! Get that?"

The maid, who really didn't look *that* much older than him, shrugged, said something in Turkish and pointed behind Trey.

"Thanks a million!" Trey turned to go, then turned back. "Anybody asks? This never happened, right?"

The maid frowned again.

"Oh, okay...sure," Trey dug into his pocket and handed her a couple of the coins his father had given him so he had some cash when he was out with Miss Renyard and the Stanhope-Leighs. "Me," he pointed to himself and shook his head, "never here, okeedoke?"

The maid took the money and Trey left her, a puzzled expression on her face, standing by the laundry basket that had without a shadow of a doubt saved his life. Going in the direction she'd pointed he found himself in an ill-lit corridor that went past a number of rooms full of people ironing, sewing, pressing and folding clothes and sheets like robots. No one looked up, no one noticed him passing by and a couple of minutes later he found himself at the requested small door.

He opened it, expecting to find himself looking at some dingy corridor, only to find that instead the door gave onto a wide boulevard, which a swift glance told him must be at the rear of the hotel. He'd been expecting to find himself somewhere *inside* the hotel and without thinking, turned to go back the way he'd come but then stopped himself. What was he thinking? This was far better than getting lost trying to find his way through the warren below stairs, on top of which, back there was where the men chasing him were, no doubt right at that moment rushing down to the basement to get him. At least he'd escaped, even if he didn't have a clue, now he had, what to do next.

As he made his way to the side of the hotel, Trey was suddenly hit by the reality of everything that had just happened. One moment he was coming back from not such a bad day spent with Arthur Stanhope-Leigh (he'd tried calling him Artie, but the boy had looked at him like he was something the dog had done), and the next his whole world had been turned upside down.

He leaned against the wall for a moment and considered what he knew for an actual fact (supposition, hunches and guesses were for the birds, as Deke Preston, PI, had put it in a recent issue of *Dime Detective*) and he had to admit that it didn't add up to much at all.

But he did know a few items of 24 carat information. To start with, somebody had been on their tail ever since they'd arrived in Constantinople, and this was *nothing* to do with his "overactive imagination" as Ahmet had also seen them; then, there was the fact that there had been a set-to in their suite, the end result of which was blood had been spilled and his father was no longer there. And finally, the bald Russian man with the gun he'd seen arguing with his father the day before had come back and ended up chasing *him*!

Trey chewed his lip nervously; whichever way you looked at it, things couldn't be much worse. But holding up a wall, moping, was not going to get anyone anywhere, least of all him. Trey squared his shoulders. It went completely against every rule in the book for a private dick to go to the police for assistance, but this wasn't a detective story, he wasn't a gumshoe and no matter how steely-eyed and iron-fisted he'd imagined he'd be, when it came to *actually* being hunted by *real* gunmen, truth was, he needed all the help he could get.

As he climbed up the steps leading to the road at the front of the hotel, a line from a recent novelette, *Time Waits For This Man*, came back to him: "A cautious guy gets to live another day", was what one of the characters had said. Trey stopped and, sticking to the wall like a gecko, he slunk the last few yards up to the corner; he wished he had a small mirror so he could use it to see what was happening without being seen, but he didn't and so very, *very* carefully he poked his head out for a swift glance.

The guy who'd written the novelette (Seymour G. Something-or-other) certainly knew his stuff when it came to survival tips. Standing right out in front of the hotel, with his back to him, was the balding man.

Trey's heart sank. He was trapped! And then a thought occurred to him...maybe it was *a* bald man, not *the* bald man. He took another quick look, this time catching the man's profile. No doubt about it, it was *the* bald man. For a moment he considered the idea of going back the way he'd come, but the last thing he felt like doing was retracing his steps. A better idea was to get away from the hotel, find somewhere reasonably out of sight where he could maybe wait for a bit to see if his dad came back, before trying his luck with the police; it was a plan, sort of. All he knew was that every instinct he owned was telling him to *get away from the Pera Palas*!

Which was all well and good, if only he could work out how to do it without being seen.

When his opportunity came he very nearly missed it because he was lost in thought trying to work out what to do. A large gaggle of people – locals, not hotel guests, from the way they were dressed – had appeared from somewhere, talking loudly and with much hand-waving.

His brain finally clicking into gear, before they'd all moved past where he was hiding Trey dashed out and just managed to bury himself within the group, who were far too busy yakking to notice him. Keeping in the middle of the crowd, he waited until he thought it was safe and then made a break for it.

There were no shouts, no pistol shots, no pounding feet chasing after him as he ran. He'd made it!

14 DISASTER!

Trey had an *extremely* rough mental map of bits of the area around the Pera Palas Hotel (basically just what he'd picked up driving with Ahmet) and, once he was totally and ab-so-*lutely* sure he wasn't being chased, he began to do what he hoped was circle back so that he could find somewhere to watch from.

Getting to where he wanted to be took a lot more time than it ought to have done because he'd ended up losing his way, which hadn't been a barrel of laughs; it was only when he recognized a Post Office his father had had Ahmet stop at the previous day that he realized he was going the wrong way. When he *eventually* managed to sort himself out with a safe spot to observe the front of the hotel, the bald man was, wouldn't you know, nowhere to be seen. And to top it all, he'd taken so long to get back that the idea of waiting to see if his father turned up didn't have a leg to stand on; hanging around any longer would just be a waste of time.

Chewing fingernails was not something Trey ever did, but he thought that now might well be the time he took the habit up...because what, apart from fret, was he going to do? His father could have been and gone for all he knew, and then there was a fact that he'd so far ignored, which was that he had *no* idea what the other guy chasing him looked like. It could be anyone. Trey's shoulders slumped, his lips pursed and his brow furrowed. He was stymied. It looked like the only thing he could do now was find a policeman and hope he spoke some English...

"Numbskull! Ignoramus! Dolt and *chump!*"

Trey shook his head and almost gave himself a personal biff. What *had* he been thinking? He should get himself straight over to the Stanhope-Leigh household! And it didn't matter that he wasn't sure *exactly* where it was, he had his father's money clip and he could get a taxi...he'd find the place somehow. Trey's right hand felt in his jacket pocket for the clip, which wasn't there, no matter how many times he felt for it, or turned the pocket out. It was gone.

With a terrible sinking feeling in his stomach Trey patted his jacket, his trousers and his jacket one last time, then stopped himself, took a deep breath and had to admit that the money clip was absolutely, one hundred and ten per cent *definitely* not there. Anywhere. At all.

"How...?" he muttered to himself. "I mean *how*?"

In his mind's eye, Trey reran where he'd been and what he'd done since he'd first stuffed the clip in his jacket, back in the suite. Could it have fallen out as he ran down the corridor? Maybe, because, as there was a man with a gun right behind him, he probably wouldn't have noticed. Had it come out as he'd plummeted down the laundry chute? More than possible, and the thought that it might have, and could at this very moment be getting laundered made him kick the wall he was standing next to. So, what was he going to do now? No money meant no taxi, and no way of getting over to the Stanhope-Leighs, wherever they were.

Okay, back to the original plan...where would be the best place to go to find a policeman?

It was as he stood, trying to remember whether he'd actually *seen* a policeman since he'd arrived in Constantinople, that Trey remembered something that had happened. When he'd gotten himself lost in the maze of narrow streets he'd encountered a group of kids who looked around his age, and he'd tried to get some directions from them. They'd seemed friendly enough, crowding round him and appearing to try and understand what he was saying, but they hadn't spoken any English and ended up kind of making fun of him. It could have happened then...one of them *might* have picked his pocket! If he was right, what a gull he'd been!

There was nothing he could do about it now, no point in trying to retrace his steps in the vain hope that he might run into those kids again. That was a pretty stupid idea, because what on earth was he going to do if he found them – take the gang on single-handed? Ask nicely for his money back? Well, you never knew, they might take pity on him. But it was beginning to get late – Trey checked his watch, which showed the time was around 7.30 – and while it wasn't getting dark yet he reckoned it wouldn't be *that* long before dusk and he did *not* want to be wandering the streets of Constantinople, alone, at night. Not if he could help it.

Setting off, Trey kept an eye out for a cop, and viewed every kid he saw with the deepest suspicion. It wasn't long before he saw that he himself was getting some pretty odd looks as he trudged the streets, and he had to admit that that was *probably* because he was lost again and was somewhere he really did not fit in at all.

And then, while he was standing on a corner, attempting to work out which of the five available directions he should take, and wondering if he'd actually been down any of the roads before, he saw the boy.

He was a little way down the road off to his left, looking his way, head cocked to one side; he was wearing grey trousers that were too big for him, cinched at the waist by a old brown leather belt, with a similarly large collarless white shirt half tucked in. He was wearing sandals instead of shoes.

But it was the shock of wiry black hair that Trey remembered. That and the more than slightly arrogant set of his face. He had been with the kids, one of whom he'd now convinced himself must have lifted his dad's money clip. He'd been hanging back, observing rather than joining in. Or maybe controlling, from a distance, what was going on? Then Trey noticed there was a girl standing behind the boy, and a couple of other kids further down the street. The gang was all here.

He had, he knew, just two choices: deal with this face to face, or walk away. And there really was no choice, because, like his gramps said, you can turn your back on a problem, but turn around again and it won't have gone away. Trey stuck his hands in his pockets and started walking.

Feeling like he should be wearing pearl-handled six-guns, leather boots with Spanish spurs and a red kerchief tied round his neck like Tom Mix, Trey came to a halt a few feet in front of the boy, who hadn't moved an inch since they'd first spotted each other. Trey raised an eyebrow and shrugged.

"Speak English?" he asked.

"Little."

"That's good."

"Why you here?"

"I think one of your friends..." Trey nodded, looking over the boy's shoulder at the other kids, who had now moved in closer, "...I think they took something off of me. A money clip."

"*My* friends?" The boy looked around, feigning surprise that there was anyone with him. "This people?"

"Yeah. *This* people."

"Was mistake."

"*Mistake?*" Trey did a double take. "How the heck can you pick a guy's pocket *by mistake*?"

The boy brushed the question aside with a wave of his hand. "You should come me. To my father house."

For a moment Trey didn't know whether to laugh or land one on the boy's nose; but, discretion being the better part of valour, he decided to save the fisticuffs for when they were really necessary. "And just *why* should I go to your father's house, huh? Tell me that, why don't you!"

"You need help."

"You think *I* need help?" Trey could feel all his frustrations coming to the boil, and, even though he knew he was outnumbered, he couldn't just *stand* there and take any more insults. He leaped forward, launching a terrific haymaker of a punch, which never landed. Trey was in mid-swing when everything stopped and he found himself held in an iron grip, his feet not touching the ground. There had been someone behind him...

The dark-haired boy, whose name was Evren, turned down yet another narrow side street, but this time he stopped almost immediately at the first door he came to. Opening it, he gestured for Trey to go in first, which he did.

There was no point in him doing anything else. Firstly, it was pitch black and he had not a single clue where he was, so making a break for it would be completely pointless. And second, even though Trey had attempted to pulp Evren's face, the boy hadn't laid a finger on him – which would have been easy enough, considering a kid about twice his size had been pinning his arms back – and he had waited until Trey had calmed down enough to talk to again.

And what he'd told Trey had made it clear he'd be stupider than a field of turnips if he *didn't* go with him. Somehow, he hadn't yet found out how, Evren knew his name, that they'd been followed, *and* that his father was no longer at the hotel!

Trey walked down a short, unlit passage with a couple of doors off it, at the end of which he could see a flight of stairs leading up to the next floor. Behind him he heard Evren talking to someone in Turkish; he glanced round to see that the girl, whom he now knew was called Neyla, had come in with them. He'd also found out that Neyla, who looked like butter wouldn't melt in her mouth, was the one who'd lifted the clip off him…"by mistake".

"Where to now?" he asked.

"Upstair."

"Who's there?"

"My father, he need you to talk to."

"Does he know where my dad is?"

Evren shrugged. "Have to ask. He hasn't tell me."

"Okay, let's ask." Trey licked his lips; he was thirsty, hungry, tired and not a little scared, but there really was no turning back. He cracked his knuckles and marched up the stairs.

From a small half landing at the top of the second flight, he saw soft lamplight, heard louder voices and caught the delicious smells spilling out of a curtained doorway. It was so inviting that his fear of the unknown melted away as he felt himself being drawn up the last few stairs as if being pulled by a magnet. At the last minute, Evren gently pushed past him and went into the room first, holding the ancient brocade curtain back.

"I have him, Baba," he said, and beckoned Trey forward with a nod of his head.

Brushing past Evren, Trey found himself in a large, gaslit room that was crammed with tables, chairs, milling people of all sizes, drying clothes, steaming pots and a number of brindle cats. In the centre of this gentle chaos sat a large, rotund man wearing shiny pinstripe trousers and matching waistcoat, an off-white shirt with the detachable collar undone, and incongruously colourful red velvet slippers. He was mopping his forehead with his half-undone dark-blue and dark-red striped tie.

"Welcome! Welcome to my most *humble* of abodes!" The man heaved himself upright and held out an enthusiastic hand, which Trey had no choice but to shake. "Duan Hendek, at your service young Drummond MacIntyre Three, terribly glad to meet you! Hatijeh…"

Evren's father turfed a cat off a nearby chair and offered it to Trey. "Sit, sit, sit! Hatijeh, wife of wives, scented everlasting love of my life, one extra for dinner!"

15 THE MYSTERY DEEPENS...

It was, in fact, more like three extra for dinner. Neyla stayed and a friend of the family turned up just as the food was being served. Evren's father, who insisted on being called Baba Duan – baba, it turned out, meaning the same as pop – couldn't have been more delighted.

Frustrated as he was at the seemingly never-ending toing and froing (exactly *how* many times did the seating arrangements have to be changed?) and the general bedlam that kept him from asking Evren's father all the questions he so *desperately* needed answers to – like how he knew his name, and where the merry heck was his money? – Trey couldn't help but be fascinated by what was going on all around him.

It turned out to be the most extraordinary meal Trey had ever eaten – the food was vibrant, exotic and spicy, much like the company – and quite unlike meals at his house which were, to say the least, quiet affairs. Evren's mother, Hatijeh, never seemed to stay in her seat for more than a minute, refilling plates, cajoling Evren's two younger brothers and baby sister, hugging her husband and attempting to engage Trey in conversation, even though she obviously didn't speak a word of English; all he could do was smile in reply, but she didn't seem to mind one bit.

At one point Trey noticed Evren looking pointedly at Neyla, who was sitting next to him; she then leaned over and quickly whispered "*Özür dilemek...sorry much...*" in his ear. Before he could respond, Hatijeh wedged herself between them and began distributing plates loaded with various desserts; when she'd finished and moved away, Trey found Neyla had swapped places with Evren's little sister and was acting like nothing had happened.

And then, all of a sudden, like the tide going out, the meal was over, the guests departed, the table cleared and the younger children packed off, Trey presumed, to bed. He was left sitting at the table with Baba Duan, Evren and Neyla.

"Tremendous!" Baba Duan patted his considerable stomach with both hands, beaming at Trey, who didn't know whether he was referring to the meal, or its effect on his waistline. "I think now is the time we should retreat to my office, as it is never good manners to discuss business at the dinner table, wouldn't you say?"

Without waiting for an answer Evren's father got up, swished the heavy curtain aside and disappeared down the stairs; Trey bit back the words "About time!" as he followed Evren and Neyla out of the room.

Baba Duan sat in an old, leather-cushioned wooden swivel chair, his back to a large roll-top desk that was stuffed to the gills with paper – actual newspapers, as well as bills, notebooks, flimsy typewritten foolscap sheets, telegrams and the odd book. There were, Trey noticed, also two tin rubbish bins on the floor overflowing with yet more screwed-up pieces of discarded paper, and as he watched Baba Duan light an aromatic, oval-shaped cigarette he found himself hoping the place never caught fire.

"So, Master T. Drummond MacIntyre Three..."

Trey held up his hand. "Can I just ask you to explain

something that's been *really* bothering me, Mr., um, Hendek?"

"It is my pleasure for you to be my guest in this matter, please to go ahead and ask!"

"How d'you know my name?"

"Explaining that is most precisely what I was *about* to do, Master T. Drummond MacIntyre Three..."

"Call me Trey, everyone does...it's, you know, easier," Trey interrupted, then glanced at Neyla and Evren. "And I'd *also* like to know where my money is..."

"So you shall, *Trey*, so you shall!" Baba Duan raised his eyebrows and smiled broadly, revealing a couple of gold teeth. "But first let *me* ask if *you* have been apologized to – this has happened, yes?" He looked from Evren to Neyla and then at Trey. "Yes?"

Trey nodded as he glanced at Neyla, who was examining her fingernails rather closely.

"It was not such a good thing that she did, the girl," Baba Duan produced the most perfect smoke ring that Trey had ever seen, and then blew a second one right through the middle of it. "But here I *have* to say to you all just how extraordinary it is, this thing *kismet*! Tremendous! Because *if* Neyla had *not* done such a bad thing, you would *not* be sitting here tonight and *I* would not be in the position of most humbly being able to try and help you. Yes?"

Trey nodded again.

"Which would have been a *bad* thing, worse than the thing that Neyla originally did. No?"

Confused, Trey did something between a shake and a nod.

"Excellent, indeed *splendid*! Now we can say *that* is all sorted out...and, where was I?"

"About to tell me how you know my name?" Trey offered.

"Yes, yes, yes! But all in the best of time." Baba Duan ground his cigarette out in a well-attended ashtray. "Your father, T. Drummond MacIntyre Two, who is he?"

"Who is he?" Trey frowned. "He's my father...what d'you mean *who is he*?? The thing *I* want to know is *where* is he?"

"An excellent question, absolutely excellent!"

"D'you know the answer?"

"It says on his card..." Baba Duan ignored Trey's question and reached into one of his capacious trouser pockets and pulled out a leather wallet, extracting a small piece of white pasteboard from it.

"Hey!" Trey leaped up off his chair. "That's my dad's business card!"

"And I think this is his, also," Baba Duan handed the money clip over to Trey, "exactly as it was 'found',

123

minus the business card that was with it. Which says that your father is –" Baba Duan patted his waistcoat until he found his half-glasses – "Senior Vice President of MacIntyre, MacIntyre and Moscowitz Engineering, of Chicago, Atlanta and New York City. And may I say, what a very *marvellous* job to have!"

"What's *that* supposed to mean?" Trey wasn't at all sure he liked the tone of voice Evren's father was now using.

"It means, I suppose, that anyone can get a card printed saying whatever they like it to say…I myself find it necessary to use a *number* of different cards in the pursuit of my own business."

A phone started to ring in the room next door, its bell sounding much like a stone being lazily rattled round a tin can. Baba Duan looked at his pocket watch, wound it a bit and put it back in his waistcoat.

"That should probably be the *Daily Register*'s New York City desk in London; Mr. Stevens approximately calls always at this hour, looking to find news to pass on across the ocean – Evren, see please what he might have to say." As Evren went, moving like a greyhound out of its trap, Baba Duan returned his attention to Trey. "You must tell me – if you please – whether your father's 'Drummond MacIntyre' name is a ruse or a ploy or some kind of – what can I say…*stratagem*? – or whether it is, in fact, real…and you *must* forgive my asking such *wretched* questions as these, but, here in Constantinople, very little is ever what it at first seems…"

"Mr. Stevens say he would like a word, Baba." Evren appeared in the doorway holding a candlestick telephone, its mouthpiece pressed to his chest; he gestured with the earpiece. "Will you?"

"When Gotham calls –" the swivel chair creaked with relief as Baba Duan got up – "I answer."

Taking the phone from his son, Baba Duan disappeared into the other room and left Trey feeling like a rug had just been pulled out from underneath him. How could this man possibly think that his father was *pretending* to be someone who he wasn't? Him too, come to that! Did it mean, for some inexplicable reason, Baba Duan thought that his father was some kind of cheap, shyster con man? He looked up, aware that Neyla and Evren were observing him, waiting for some kind of reaction, aware also that they must be wondering if he was a liar or not.

"I *am* who I say I am!" Trey could feel his ears reddening. "And I don't care if you believe me or not…" He got up, willing himself to stand as tall and straight as he could. "Now I have my belongings back, give me directions to the hotel and I won't be any more trouble to you, or your father."

"Please to sit down, Trey."

Trey hadn't noticed Baba Duan had come back into the room.

"What, so's I can listen to you spout some more baloney about my father? I've had enough of an earful of *that* already."

"A thousand apologies, and more..." Baba Duan returned to his long-suffering chair, which complained quietly to itself as he lit another cigarette and leaned backwards. "In this city it pays handsomely *never* to take anything, or anyone, at the value of their face, Trey. It may seem a poor show, coming from a place where people are very much proud of being men of their word, but this is Constantinople! We *always* expect there to be a number of versions of every story – a Turkish one, naturally, an English one, a German, Russian or an Italian, or even an *American* one – any of which might turn out to be true!"

"So are you saying that you now believe my father is who he says he is?" Baba Duan nodded. "Terrific – what changed your mind?"

"The admirable Mr. Stevens, working, as he does, for the *Daily Register*'s London office, was able to confirm with alacrity that MacIntyre, MacIntyre and Moscowitz is indeed an *entirely* reputable company..."

"I coulda *told* you my father would check out!" Trey

grinned widely, an odd sense of relief making him feel almost light-headed – of *course* his father was who he said he was!

"Well, I haven't known you for a time that is long enough to trust you – and my family would never have enough to eat if I believed *everything* anyone of such a short acquaintance told me." Dragon-like, Baba Duan blew smoke out of his nostrils. "And as you have so recently witnessed, my family, and friends, have gloriously healthy appetites."

"D'you trust me enough to tell me what the heck is going on? I mean, I can see how you found out my dad's name, but what about mine?"

"I know a lot more than that...including that your esteemed father has been of much interest to certain people, and that he is no longer to be found in his rooms at the Pera Palas."

Trey frowned, and he leaned forward. "Yeah, I know you know, but *how* do you know? And where is my father now, and what can I do?" Trey stood up, like his chair had burst into flame. "I...I should go to the police! That's what I was trying to do when I met them," he indicated Evren and Neyla. "The police'll help me find him!"

"Please take the seat once more." Baba Duan waved calming hands at Trey. "In my most modest opinion it would be unwise in the most extreme to go to the police…"

"Why?" Trey looked angrily puzzled, but did sit back down.

"They generally truly know very little that is useful."

"The police?"

Baba Duan nodded. "Unlike myself, the police do not like to pay for information, so do not get told very much. My business is the news business, young Master Trey, and I am pretty fairly good at it. In fact, *sometimes* I know what the story is going to be even before it happens!" Two phones began ringing at the same time in the other room and Evren was out of his chair before Baba Duan managed to even lift an eyebrow in his general direction. "I have people, they bring me scraps of information, from here and from there – a lot of people, including my son, and his friends." He smiled at Neyla. "They supply me with the fresh ingredients, and I, the *chef*, cook the story and sell slices of it to my customers. Your father's return to Constantinople – such a fuss with the luggage! – was one such particle, as was the fact that it was noticed that you were being followed. Add them together and you have, mmm –" Baba Duan licked his lips – "maybe a taste of something about to happen? Certainly a dish very worthy of keeping the eye on."

Evren appeared in the doorway, clasping two phones to himself with one hand and holding the earpieces in the other. "From London, Baba...*Daily Telegraph* and *Daily Mirror*. What to do?"

"One moment, Trey, quite very possibly two..."

That had been the last Trey had seen of Baba Duan, who he could still hear talking away, nineteen to the dozen in the other room, as he was led back upstairs by Evren. Disappointed. Irritated. Scuttled. Aggravated (and how!). He'd felt all those things, and he'd wanted to scream "Answer *my* questions first!", but had known it wouldn't have gotten him anywhere.

And now here he was, lying in the makeshift bed that had been put together for him by Evren and his mother: a thin mattress, a soft cotton sheet folded over and a pillow, on the floor in the room where he'd eaten dinner. It sure as heck was not the Pera Palas, but he felt safe, as it seemed somehow very unlikely that anyone was going to bust in and try and take him off who knew where.

As he lay on his back, waiting for sleep to pull the shades down over his eyes, his mind raced as he thought about his day; everything that had happened (so much of it!) was all jumbled up and kind of out of order –

nearly being caught in the laundry chute...meeting Evren and the sticky-fingered Neyla...the blood on the floor of their suite...getting lost...the fortuitously soft landing in the basement. And then there was what Evren had told him as he'd taken him upstairs – about his father being bundled into a black sedan and driven away from the back of the hotel, according to one of Baba Duan's informants who'd apparently witnessed the event. Plus there was also the comment about his father's "return" to Constantinople.

Trey sat up. He should go right back downstairs now and ask Baba Duan for some answers! He yawned and rubbed his gritty eyes. Then again, he was bushed. He could demand some action *first thing tomorrow!* Baba Duan had mentioned going to the American Consulate, which seemed like a neat idea, so he'd insist on going there straight away – maybe after finding out more about this nonsense concerning his father having been to the city before, as he was pretty darn positive this was the first time *either* of them had been to the place. But for now he was going to stop trying to figure out the unfigurable, as one of the private eyes had said in a story he'd read called *The Toughest Nut.*

Instead, he thought about Baba Duan's job. He'd told him he worked as what he called a "stringer", a reporter who supplied stories to foreign newspapers. In Baba

Duan's case it was rather more complicated than that because *he* worked for a number of papers, all of whom he had somehow managed to convince he was doing so exclusively ("They pay *nothing*, these people...but they pay a *bigger* nothing if they think you work for no one else"). And it seemed like there were two papers in New York, two in London, one in Berlin, Germany, and one in Paris, France, all of whom were under the distinct impression they had their very own, individual correspondent in Constantinople.

To maintain this illusion, Baba Duan had a number of phone lines (a "sensational" feat in itself, requiring very large amounts of bribery and palm-greasing to pull off, apparently) and then for each of his clients he operated with a different name. Hence his need for a selection of business cards. It brought to mind an act Trey had seen once on a visit to the circus, a man rushing about, desperately trying to keep plates spinning on the end of bamboo poles.

As he drifted off Trey wondered how on earth you could keep a racket this complicated going without being driven completely screwy; although, he thought, you'd have to look pretty darned hard to find a more relaxed and happy person than Baba Duan – but then *his* father wasn't missing, quite possibly kidnapped, and *he* wasn't lying on some strange kitchen floor trying to figure out what to do next...Trey sat bolt upright again. Check the hotel! He *must* check the hotel to see if his father had come back and this whole thing was a horrible misunderstanding! As he lay back down, it occurred to him that he'd be in trouble the like of which he'd never been in before if he'd got everything completely wrong. He couldn't have...could he...?

16 ...AND THE PLOT THICKENS

Trey awoke with a start, light streaming in through the room's unshuttered windows along with the eerie, almost other-worldly wail from a nearby mosque that heralded the beginning of a new day in Constantinople. He recalled, because his father had told him all about it on their first morning in the city, that this was a *muezzin*, "...the person who calls the faithful to prayers at the mosque, something which he will do, without fail, five times a day, every day; interestingly, in the past, son, he was often a blind man..."

* * *

The hurly-burly of breakfast stopped him from doing anything about suggesting the hotel was checked. After it was over and cleared away, Baba Duan – looking exactly the same as the night before, right down to what looked like an identical tie, but now cleaned, pressed and tidy – stayed at the table reading a newspaper; Trey went and sat next to him as he took his first sips of coffee from a tiny, delicate bone-china cup which, in his hand, looked like it should be in his daughter's tea set.

"I meant to ask you last night…"

Baba Duan looked over his half glasses. "Ask what about, young gentleman?"

"Two things…you said that my father was coming *back* here to Constantinople, right?"

"And what the question number one is?" Baba Duan put his paper down and sat back in his chair.

"What did you mean? 'Cos we neither of us – cross my heart and hope to die – have *ever* been here before, Mr. Baba Duan, sir."

"You know completely *every*where your esteemed father has been to?"

"No, sir, but I do know he's not a liar! He told me this was going to be some trip because he'd never been out of the country before, just like me."

"Well…" Baba Duan stuck his lower lip out, raised

his eyebrows and nodded to himself; then he got up. "Come with me. I have something you really should must see…"

Baba Duan led the way downstairs, through his main office and into the room with the telephones in it (they sat on a long table, with pieces of card that had the details and particulars of all the different newspapers thumb-tacked to the wall behind). At the rear of the room Trey noticed there was a door with a bare light bulb over it, which was glowing red; as he was about to ask what it meant the light went out and the door opened, revealing Evren, his sleeves rolled up and wearing a green eyeshade, like the ones Trey had seen newsmen wear in the movies.

"I have develop, Baba…" he said, wiping his hands on a grubby cloth. "Just wait the negative to dry."

Behind Evren Trey could see a room full of equipment and what he could now see were photographic prints strung from wires like washing on a line.

"This boy! Such talent – he take the picture, he *make* the picture!" Baba Duan beamed, his arms outstretched. "Where is the one from before, Evren, the one I think we should now show to our very good visitor and guest?"

"In the file, Baba…the Almanya file."

"Germany, of course, of course…" Baba Duan turned on his heels and went back into his office, waving a finger in the air. "One moment, Trey, or maybe two…"

"You take pictures?" Trey asked; Evren nodded. "Is this your darkroom – can I see?"

"Yes, please," Evren smiled, standing aside to let Trey in. "You have camera?"

Trey shook his head as he went into the small room. "I was planning on asking for one this next Christmas."

"Christmas?"

"You know…" Trey gazed around at what seemed more like a laboratory, and certainly smelled like one. "Santa Claus and stuff?"

"We not have."

"Oh…really?" Trey's attention was drawn to a by-no-means brand-new camera; its leatherette covering peeling and scuffed, the creases in its bellows worn from use, it sat on a bench ready to take pictures. "That yours?"

Evren nodded. "Kodak Series III, version No. 2C." The boy shrugged. "One day I will have Leica, maybe Zeiss, but I am good with this."

"He most genuinely is!" Baba Duan appeared at the door. "A small fragment of your time, Trey…I have something you should see, a very truly anomalous event, I think you will find yourself agreeing. Maybe there is some explanation, who can tell?"

Baba Duan led Trey back to his office and pointed to

his desk, which Trey saw had been cleared somewhat. In the empty space there were two ten-by-eight inch, black and white photographs.

"See if you recognize," Baba Duan said, waving Trey forward.

He walked over to the desk and looked at the grainy images that had been printed onto the glossy paper; they were of the same smartly-dressed man. In the one on the left he was alone, dressed in a dark pinstripe suit and what looked to be brogues, standing in a street, a newspaper tucked under one arm as he lit a cigarette; he had been looking towards the photographer when that picture had been taken. In the second the man was in a plain suit and getting out of a car, the door being held open by a man who couldn't be anyone else but their driver, Ahmet.

In both of the pictures Trey found himself staring at his father. He blinked, glanced over at Baba Duan and Evren, who were observing him quizzically and with interest, and then back at the picture. "So?"

"Evren took this very picture, the one with the car, yesterday." Baba Duan smiled. "And he took the one other one about nearly four weeks ago. Here in Constantinople, on the Grand Rue de Pera."

"But..." Trey shot a glance at the pictures. "But that's not possible..."

"I very much assure that this is what did happen."

"You say! But *we* were still in London four weeks ago." Trey looked at the pictures again, and it was still his father looking back at him.

Or was it...?

Trey picked up the pinstriped shot, examined it closely and then held it at a distance. He got a feeling there was something not quite right about it, but he couldn't, for the life of him, put a finger on what that was. Then he realized it wasn't what his father *looked* like, so much as what he was *wearing*...as far as he knew his father didn't own a pinstripe suit, and, come to think of it, wouldn't *ever* wear brogues! *And* his hair looked shiny, as if it might have been brilliantined. His mother did *not* approve of brilliantine.

"This one is *not* my father." Trey put the picture back on the desk and folded his arms.

"If *you* say that is so...but I am very strongly interested in why you seem so quite positive it is *not* your much-admired father."

"It sure *looks* like him...had me fooled there for a moment...but it isn't, Baba Duan, honest. The clothes are all wrong, and my mother wouldn't let him in the house if he put oil on his hair, believe me. And like I say, we hadn't even left for Constantinople when it was taken." Trey shrugged apologetically at Evren, hoping the boy didn't think he was accusing him of lying. "Maybe it's just a trick of the light, right?"

Baba Duan held out his hand and Evren gave him a sheaf of photos. "A trickiness of light *every* time?" he asked, handing the photos to Trey.

Slowly leafing through the half-dozen pictures, there was no way Trey could deny that in every single one of them the man did look just like his father. Except for the clothes. "I don't understand..."

"This is also true for myself. It is what the French call *une énigme*, a great puzzlement – how can this person be in two place at actually the identical time? There are no possibilities!"

"Well *I'm* not lying!"

"And neither, Evren says to me, does his camera." Baba Duan looked at his son for confirmation.

"If you are honest with it, Baba, the camera give you back what is real."

"But why were you following this man? What's with all the pictures?"

"Sit down, I will explain..."

Before he did, Baba Duan sent Evren off to arrange for the provision of fresh coffee, pastries, and his cigarettes; then he turned to Trey, his ever-present smile replaced by an expression somewhere between stern and thoughtful. Trey didn't know what he was going to say, but he had a very definite feeling that he wasn't going to like it much.

"You first and most foremostly should understand that rumour is the air in this city's lungs, and intrigue is very correctly said to be its lifeblood. I can tell you this with my eye on heaven –" Baba Duan looked upwards, a comically pious expression on his face to emphasize his point – "knowing it to be completely the truth. Possibly the *only* truth. You *must* comprehend this because, in Constantinople, deciding which 'facts' are indeed not facts, but fiction, and quite how much of the 'truth' you are being told has been bent to suit the teller, it is a way of life. Do you see?"

"Yeah, I suppose..." Trey frowned, unable to work out why he was being told any of this.

"Do you play poker, young Drummond MacIntyre Three?"

"Me? No."

"A pity. Then you would understand most terrifically. I will 'cut to the chase', as I have read they say in the motion pictures business. The rumours concerning this man –" Baba Duan picked up one of the pictures – "are that he is a spy..."

"You think my father's a *spy*?"

At that moment Evren came back into the room carrying a brass coffee tray with cups and small glasses of water on it, followed by his mother, Hatijeh, with a tray of pastries, and one of his brothers who had the cigarettes and matches.

"Excuse...no, the wrong picture altogether – you see how confusing this two people are?" Baba Duan put the photo of Trey's father down and picked up one of the man who looked just like him. "But I *know* that *this* man, the name he uses is Gessler..." Baba Duan took something with a lot of pistachios on it off the tray as Hatijeh went past him. "*He* is a spy. I am pretty much darn sure of that."

"Gessler?" Trey took the cup and saucer that Evren gave him without paying much attention to what he was doing.

"I *think* probably for Almanya, or maybe Rusya – for the Germany or the Russia..." The pastry disappeared from view. "...Maybe both. Sip your coffee s-l-o-w-l-y, my young United States friend. Take your time."

"What?" Trey looked down, surprised to see what he was holding; he'd had coffee before and wasn't all that sure he wanted to repeat the experience, but on the other hand did not want to appear rude. "Oh...right..."

"But now I have a confusion about this man." Baba Duan took his own advice and sipped his coffee. "And be sure to drink *only* the top half of it all...the rest even a goat might not eat."

Trey did as he was advised, surprised by the rich, aromatic smell of the dark, slightly bitter (but then again quite *sweet*) liquid, which tasted nothing like the coffee he'd had back home in Chicago. Which is when he remembered he hadn't asked his second question, about checking the hotel...

"Your baba," said Evren, before Trey could open his mouth, "he have brother?"

"One *hundred* per cent!" Baba Duan lit himself a congratulatory cigarette, as if celebrating his son's genius. "On the button of the nose, fruit of my loins! *Do* you have an uncle, Trey?"

"Yeah, I do."

"There!"

"He's my *mother's* brother. Six inches shorter than my father, and with fair hair."

"Ah..."

"Look, whether you believe me or not, I'm telling you that that guy in the pinstripe suit is *not* my dad, or my uncle, or *anything* to do with my family!"

"I am prepared to say that *I* possibly believe you are very much precisely right..." Baba Duan leaned back in his chair and spent a moment watching the curling, grey silk snake flowing from the tip of his oval-shaped cigarette as it poured upwards, seemingly in defiance of gravity. "But the problem is, young Trey, just how will your acclaimed father convince those who have taken him that they do not possess the right person – the spy I think *they* think they have taken – when, here in this city, a man is hardly *ever* who he says he is?" In the other room one of the phones started to ring. "Indeed, just like my good self..."

Trey watched him walk out of the room, his second question still unasked and unanswered.

17 ON THE MOVE

As Trey waited for Baba Duan and Evren to deal with whatever business the phone call was all about, Hatijeh came bustling back into the outer office, drying her hands on a dishcloth and bringing with her the smell of something good she must have been cooking upstairs. As she began collecting the coffee cups she reached out to pick up Trey's and instead put the saucer on top of the cup and turned it over; head on one side, she smiled gently at him and nodded, putting a small coin on top of the cup before busying herself with the rest of the clearing up. Trey knew that she didn't speak any English, so he smiled back at her, wondering why on Earth she'd made more mess by upending his cup. And exactly what was with the coin?

Just then Baba Duan came out of what Trey now thought of as the phone room and there was a flurry of conversation and hand-waving with his wife, which it didn't take Trey long to figure out had something to do with him, and, oddly, his coffee cup.

In mid-sentence Baba Duan switched from Turkish to English and turned to Trey. "You are in luckiness!"

"I am? Why?"

"Because my illustrious wife *very* much desires to tell the story of your coffee!" Baba Duan gestured rather grandly at Trey's upturned cup as if it was truly an object to be marvelled at. "She feel you have, how shall I say...sadness and desolation, and it might tell you something."

"*What* might tell me something – I drank my coffee."

"But..." Baba Duan bent down and picked Trey's cup up to reveal the intricate, lacy pattern the grounds had left behind as they'd drained out, "...this receptacle is a book, and my Hatijeh a *magnificent* reader of its pages!"

* * *

Hatijeh had claimed she could see fireworks, a black cat and a rat in the bottom left-hand side of the cup, which, she had said through Baba Duan, meant Trey's recent past had included him having problems with a dark and unpredictable thief. Considering what he assumed she must know about his present circumstances, this, Trey considered, was not what he would call hot news.

Hatijeh continued the reading with what the future would hold and according to the signs in the top half of the cup, it was a lot brighter. An open window pointed to a streak of fortune, a man on a horse was good news and strong lines denoted a successful journey. Baba Duan was delighted with the results, expressing his undying respect for his wife's clairvoyant talents, and although Trey was less than amazed by the quality of the fortune telling, he thanked Hatijeh anyway. Like his gramps said, it didn't cost a dime to be polite, and it might earn you a dollar.

"And now I very much am of the opinion, Trey, that the time has come to do as I said..." Baba Duan straightened his tie.

"What was that?"

"The journey you must take – at the *first* available opportunity – is to the premises of your inestimable American Consulate!"

"I never went there with my dad. Where is it?"

"Not so terrifically far away, in fact entirely near to the Pera Palas, where you were staying! Evren and Neyla will take you – Evren!" Baba Duan snapped his fingers, making a sound like a cracker being pulled. "Neyla!"

Trey was used to pretty cut and dried farewells, which required of you no more than a firm handshake and some courteous, well-mannered small talk about how marvellous it had all been. Getting out of Evren's house was nothing like that. It took what seemed like hours, necessitating him being hugged more than once by every member of the household, as well as a couple of people he'd never seen before.

"It has been our most sublime pleasure to be the recipients of your company, young Master Drummond MacIntyre Three!" Baba Duan held the door open to let Trey, Evren and Neyla out. "I would of course myself escort *your* good self to the Consulate, but I have an engagement of some great importance that I must attend to with *immediacy*. Business is business, as I'm sure your father would ultimately understand."

Trey nodded, thinking that Baba Duan and his father more than likely had completely different ideas about what the word "business" meant, and was then completely taken aback when Hatijeh looked at him, burst into tears and had to be taken off to be calmed down by a neighbour. Watching her go he did wonder if she'd been completely truthful about what she'd seen in his coffee grounds. But he had no time to think about that as, finally, the front door closed behind him and he was on his way.

Moments after Evren, Trey and Neyla had disappeared down the street on their way to the Consulate, a mud-spattered, travel-strained Opel roadster, its top down, pulled up outside the house. A bearded man got out and stretched very slowly, as if he'd been sitting in the same position for rather longer than was comfortable; he was dressed in dark brown corduroy trousers and a tweed jacket, dark glasses and a broad-brimmed hat which, bending down to look in the wing mirror, he carefully adjusted. The man reached back into the car for a gabardine coat and a leather briefcase, which he tucked under one arm; he then walked round the car and went up the steps to the front door, rapping imperiously on it with a leather-gloved knuckle.

The door opened, the space completely filled by Baba Duan's impressive bulk. "A very fine and good morning?" Baba Duan said, staring inquiringly at the man, looking him up and down.

"*Nicht unbedingt*...not, I think, necessarily," the man

replied curtly, his accent guttural and clipped. "I would like to come in. *Sofort!* Now!"

"I am so very much afraid that I was myself just on my way out – an errand of some small importance. I will naturally of course be back…" Baba Duan caught sight of the gun barrel pointing out from under the raincoat the man had over his right arm. "Ah, yes…I can now see that I am about to be somewhat unavoidably delayed…"

"Correct."

Baba Duan stood to one side and waved the man into the house. "*Kommen Sie herein*, as I recall that you say it in Berlin."

"You have a good memory, Herr Hendek." The man followed Baba Duan as he backed down the corridor towards his office. "I hope it is good enough."

"Good enough for what, could I possibly ask?"

"You will find out, soon enough." The man closed the office door behind them; putting down his briefcase and raincoat he locked the door and then waved the Luger automatic pistol at Baba Duan. "Sit down."

Doing as he'd been instructed, Baba Duan leaned back in his chair and, his eyes never leaving the man's face, reached into a pocket of his capacious jacket. "Cigarettes…" he explained, bringing out a packet. "For my nerves."

"You are nervous, Herr Hendek?"

"Not precisely at the moment..." Baba Duan struck a match, his hand shaking slightly. "...But I very much believe quite firmly that prevention is better than needing a cure."

"A wise principle, to be sure."

"Indeed," echoed Baba Duan, failing, for the first time in a long time, to blow the perfect smoke ring. "What can I do for you, Mr. Herr Reinhardt Gessler?"

"Ah..." Gessler smiled thinly, touching his bearded chin. "You have seen through this, how shall I say, this *theatrical* disguise."

Baba Duan raised his eyebrows. "You are, how shall *I* say, very close up to me."

"And yet, as far as *I* know, we have never met."

"True. But it is my job to have knowledge."

"We are more the same than we are different, you and I...how did you get this knowledge – or was it a shot in the dark?" Gessler swung the Luger to and fro.

"As you say, we have similarities. I collect information, like you."

"Except *I* have one master, and you have many."

"That is where yourself and I have taken our own roads, Herr Gessler."

"Correct." Gessler pulled up a chair and sat right in front of Baba Duan, the pistol mere inches away from his stomach. "But our roads have now met and I require you to tell me the answers to the questions I am about to ask."

"And if I cannot find these answers?"

"If you have been doing your job as well as it appears you have, you will know enough about me to understand that I have the ways and the means," Gessler paused and glanced at his briefcase, "to give you whatever help you might need, Herr Hendek. Would you like me to go into more detail? I always carry a few pictures with me…"

Baba Duan smiled rather too broadly, extracting an off-white handkerchief from his trousers and dabbing his upper lip. "That will not, I think, under the circumstances, be at all necessary."

"I do hope not." Gessler looked at his watch. "I do not have so much time."

"What could I possibly know that you do not already?"

"Tell me about the American and his son. Tell me *everything* you know…"

"Would it not be quicker, if your time is of an essential nature, for *you* to tell *me* what you know, and I will do my absolute level best to fill in the spaces left over?"

Gessler's right hand whipped out like a snake, the barrel of the gun slashing across Baba Duan's ear.

"I obviously did not make myself as clear as I had intended: I said 'tell me *everything*', Herr Hendek. *Und schnell* – quickly!"

A bright redness grew on the handkerchief which Baba Duan held tightly to the side of his face. He licked his lips and fumbled for another cigarette, Gessler taking a lighter from his coat pocket, leaning over and flicking it into life...

Hardly more than five minutes after arriving, Herr Reinhardt Gessler exited Baba Duan's house. He strode quickly to his car and drove off at some speed, leaving behind a sluggish cloud of oily exhaust smoke and dust.

In his office, blood still flowing from the gash on his ear, Baba Duan Hendek remained sitting in his chair, staring at his desk. He had never considered himself an especially brave man – or a particularly bad one, either – but even he was surprised at how quickly threats of violence against his person had forced him to hand over everything he knew about the Drummond MacIntyres, Two and Three. Well, *almost* everything he knew.

What had incensed Baba Duan was Gessler's promise that he would return and reduce the house – and all who lived inside – to ashes if he discovered he hadn't been told the truth about anything. What had his family got to do with this business? Nothing! Except maybe for Evren, but he was only doing what he was told, so that didn't count.

One of the phones rang in the other room and Baba Duan got a little unsteadily to his feet. The truth was that what he had failed to tell Gessler was not a fact – it was not something he *knew*, but a suspicion, a theory... a guess. And therefore, Baba Duan smiled thinly to himself, it was not something the German spy wanted to know, was it.

18 SO NEARLY THERE

As Trey followed Evren and Neyla, he found himself going through narrow alleys (where the top storeys of some of the houses almost touched), across wide, crowded boulevards and then, at a turn, into the awning-covered warren of a market. Here the intensity of colours – brilliant jewellery in one shop window, next to jewel-like fruit and vegetables displayed as if they had all just tumbled, freshly picked, out of a "horn of plenty" – collided with the tapestry of aromas from fishmongers, *perfumiers*, spice merchants, coffee houses and restaurants.

They were passing a bakery when Trey spotted a boy bringing a tray of sesame-covered bread sticks out into the shop; they looked so very tasty that Trey allowed himself a moment's pause in the mission and gave Evren the money to pay for some. Handed over and wrapped in a sheet of thin paper, they were still warm, and smelled and tasted as delicious as they looked. The sesame seeds tumbling like large grains of sand to the ground, Trey chivvied his new friends to hurry up and get him to the American Consulate.

"So you have not been this place before?" Evren halted for a moment at a water fountain, its brass spigot turned a dark, mottled green by verdigris, cupped his hands and took a drink.

"No..." Trey, who was too thirsty to care about all the warnings his mother had given him about drinking the water "on the Continent" before she left for Los Angeles, waited for Neyla to finish, then took his turn. "My dad got some introductions when we were in London – to this English family, the Stanhope-Leighs?" Trey shrugged and sighed. "They have kids kind of my age, and a tutor, and Ahmet – the guy driving the car in your photographs? – he took me over there a couple of times when my dad had to work. We did this and that."

"'*This and that*' not good?" asked Evren.

"It was okay, I suppose." Trey nodded to himself,

having to allow that Arthur was not quite the *complete* milquetoast he'd first thought. "But I'd've rather been with my father, this being a holiday and all."

"The childs were not so nice?" Evren asked.

"Arthur and Christine? They were okay, like I said." Trey saw Neyla staring at him, frowning like she couldn't work him out. "Look, they were *fine*, I just didn't want to *be* there, that was all! I go away with my father and all I do is get to spend time with strangers..."

"We strangers." It was Neyla's turn to shrug.

Coming round a bend in the road, Trey's spirits lifted when he saw "Old Glory", the Stars and Stripes, waving from the top of a flagpole a couple of hundred yards up the street – he was nearly home! Sort of. Trey stopped walking, aware that the adventure was almost over and that he probably wouldn't ever see Evren and Neyla again; he looked up and saw that the two of them were a little way ahead of him. He was about to catch them up and tell them that it was different with them, that he somehow didn't think *they* were strangers, but he never got the chance.

None of them saw the two-door Opel roadster coming. Seemingly from out of nowhere it just appeared from behind Trey, screeching to a halt just ahead of him, one of its front tyres up on the pavement and its mud-splattered bonnet angled to create a barrier between him and the other two. A man jumped up from the passenger seat, making Trey think that the car looked like it was some kind of giant mobile Jack-in-a-box and the man should be on springs.

But he wasn't. And the half-smile was wiped off Trey's face as the man leaped to the pavement and he started to lunge towards him. But the fact that this was not an accident – that it was actually *all about him* – was something Trey figured out too late to do anything about. Momentarily rooted to the spot, he finally turned to make a run for it as a bearded man, wearing dark glasses and a hat, dashed from the driver's side; he said something in a language Trey could have sworn was German.

The next thing Trey knew was that some thick, coarse cloth had been tied over his eyes and someone had grabbed him from behind, picking him up as if he weighed next to nothing. Then a rope or a belt was pulled tight around him, pinning his arms down, and whoever was carrying him dropped him like a brick. Lying, dazed and in complete darkness, Trey heard a slamming noise right above his head. They'd put him in the trunk! The car rocked as the two men got in and, as the driver hit the throttle, it roared off down the street.

* * *

It had all happened so fast neither Evren or Neyla could quite believe what they'd just witnessed – Trey was actually in the back of the car they could now see skidding sideways and disappearing from sight!

The only signs that anything had happened, apart from the fact that Trey really was no longer with them, were the skid marks on the pavement and the nose-pricking smell of overheated rubber. The street was oddly silent, almost as if the buildings, and everyone in them, were holding their breath, shocked by what had occurred.

Evren looked around, waiting for someone who had witnessed the incident to react; there were a scattering of other people on the street, but by the way they were acting none of them appeared to have seen or heard anything. He looked at Neyla, wondering how that could possibly be, and shook his head. "That man, the one with the beard...he was foreign, but what kind?"

Neyla shrugged. "Baba Duan's not going to be pleased we didn't get him safely to the Consulate..."

"We shan't tell him."

"No?"

"No, this is *our* job and we must finish it!"

"What *can* we do?"

"We must tell the Americans." Evren pointed up the road at the Consulate.

"They will listen to *us*?" Neyla looked down at her threadbare, workaday clothes, her grubby hands and scuffed shoes.

"You're right..." Evren thought for moment, chewing on a nail. "But there are other people, people they *will* listen to."

"People *we* know?"

"We don't know them yet."

"You mean the English?" Neyla frowned. "How?"

"We have to find the driver first: Ahmet, the one who took Trey to the house. He knows where these people live."

"How many Ahmets must there be in Constantinople who drive cars, Evren? How many?"

Evren took something out of his trouser pocket and held it up. "Only one who looks like this," he said, showing Neyla one of the photographs he'd taken of Trey's father and his chauffeur...

Tied up and blindfolded in the boot of the car, Trey tried to somehow wedge his shoulders and legs against something in an attempt to stop himself from being thrown about like a sack of potatoes. Something, he had to admit, he was not able to do with any great success.

It felt as if the driver was succeeding in an attempt to

find every single pothole in Constantinople as the car bounced like crazy – and Trey bounced with it – down hills, round bends and across what felt like rutted fields. None of this in any way helped Trey collect his thoughts and try to understand what had happened to him; he'd never seen either of the people in the car before and could only imagine they must have something to do with The Bald-headed Man. Which meant that he *could* be being taken off to the same place his father was being kept.

Maybe.

But what if it was someone else, someone working *against* The Bald-headed Man? What if he was being used as a bargaining chip? Give us the father, or we'll kill the kid, that kind of thing? Or...Trey forced all the "what if" thoughts away and concentrated on hoping that Evren and Neyla were doing something to help him.

When the car did screech to a halt, flinging Trey backwards and forwards so fast he actually did see stars, he was sure he could hear the sort of sounds you'd kind of associate with boats: the slapping of water against wood, the creak of taughtened ropes, the discordant yell of seagulls. They hadn't, he realized, actually driven *that* far, the journey had just seemed never-ending. Did that mean they were either down by the Bosphorus, or over on the northern side of the Golden Horn? It could only be one or the other, if he recalled the map in the guidebook correctly. Then the trunk was opened and all the sounds got louder and a small amount of light seeped through the coarse weave of the sacking.

"You let me go!" Trey yelled, kicking out blindly. "GET ME OUT OF HERE!"

"*Sei ruhig, Junge* – be quiet, boy!" said a harsh voice, as hands gripped Trey painfully tight and held him down. "It will hurt so very much more if I have to *make* you do as I say. Stanislaus, get the case, please."

Trey heard footsteps walk away, now completely sure the men who had grabbed him were German (they sounded just like the Grünestadts, who owned the shoe store his mother took him to), but no nearer working out why they'd done it. As the seconds ticked by the man who'd spoken continued holding him down with an uncomfortably iron grip, and then he heard the other person returning and the sound of latches unsnapping and hinges creaking. Without warning Trey felt himself being rolled sideways out of the car's trunk and into something else; he had no idea what it was, except that it was even smaller and more cramped that where he'd been. Then the hinges creaked, everything went dark again and the latches snapped shut.

He was in some kind of case!

He was in some kind of case that was being lifted and carried off...but where to? Were they going to throw him in the water and get rid of him? The thought that he might be moments from drowning made panic rise in him like heat from a flame and as Trey began to struggle the case was put down.

"I rarely warn people twice, *junge* Herr MacIntyre." The man's voice was muffled by the case. "I recommend you stay calm, and this part of your journey will all very soon be over."

Stay calm! Trey could hardly believe his ears! Here he was, tied up like Houdini – locked in a *box*! – and he was supposed to stay *calm*?

"I shall take your silence as an agreement that you will make no more trouble."

Somehow the man did not sound to Trey like he was about to dump him in the Bosphorus, so he decided to keep his mouth shut. For now. The men grunted and the case was lifted up again, and he could hear that they were much nearer the water. And then he became aware that something had changed and they weren't on solid ground any more...the case he was in was jerkily swinging to and fro, the water sounding *very* near now. Where the heck were they taking him? A boat? That had to be it... but a boat that was going to take him exactly where?

Before he could take the thought any further, Trey heard a lot more grunting and he could tell, just knew, that he was being manhandled *into* something, rather than *onto* a boat. The case he'd been stuffed in was roughly dropped. For a moment there was silence, and then he heard the muffled sound of a loud, harsh coughing. He knew that sound! He knew he'd heard it very recently, but where?

And then it came to him: Venice.

It was the noise of a rotary-engined plane firing up. That was it! He'd been dumped, like a piece of luggage, on a seaplane that was about to take off, taking him with it – this was *not* how he'd imagined his first flight! So much for helping get his father back, he thought to himself as the engine roared into life and the plane began to move...

19 MAKING PLANS

It was early evening when the black Citroën B12 pulled up outside a rather grand house, lights burning in most of the windows. It had taken a *lot* longer than Evren had thought it would to find the right Ahmet, the only one who could help him put his plan into action.

"This is the place, where I bring the young Mr. Trey," Ahmet said over his shoulder.

"I think it would be good...much better, I think... if you came with us." Now they were actually *at* their destination, Evren could see there were almost as many holes in this "plan" as there were in his mother's tea-strainer.

"*Us?*" hissed Neyla. "*Me?*"

"But I..."

"I will come with you." Ahmet opened his door and got out of the car. "I had the feeling something was not right when I went to pick up Mr. Macktire this morning; they told me at the hotel that he was suddenly not there any longer. Trey had told me a man had been there with a gun. And now *you* tell me about what happened to *him*, and I think it's true that he *and* his father are now both in trouble. We should tell these people." He nodded towards the house. "The *effendi* must know them well to bring his son here."

Evren shot Neyla a glance, inwardly sighing with relief as he stepped down onto the pavement. He actually didn't blame her for being scared about going up to the house; the idea of standing there on his own when the door opened – of trying to explain, in his bad English, what had happened – made him feel the size of an ant. He knew all about how rich foreigners (rich Turkish people, for that matter) looked down at those they thought were beneath them.

Rather than be left behind on her own in the car, Neyla followed Evren, but stayed at the bottom of the steps, watching Ahmet use the polished brass bell-pull.

Somewhere inside the house they could hear a muffled ringing, and they waited. And waited. And just as Ahmet was about to ring the bell again the door finally opened.

"May I be of assistance?" The words were out of the butler's mouth before he'd fully taken in that he was addressing what appeared to be someone's driver, who was accompanied by one...no, two slightly untidy children. He cleared his throat. "Are you quite sure that you have the *correct* residence?"

"This is Stanhope-Leigh, yes?" enquired Ahmet politely.

"Quite so..." the butler began to shut the door. "But I'm sure we have no need for whatever it is that you are selling."

"Not sell," Ahmet's foot shot out and blocked the door. "This about Mr. Macktire."

"And Trey," added Evren. "There is trouble!"

"I really am *very* sorry, but Mr. and Mrs. Stanhope-Leigh are out at present and as far as I know you will find Mr. MacIntyre, and his son, at the Pera Palas Hotel. *Not* here." The butler forcefully moved to close the door, only to find it, equally forcefully, being pushed back. "Now look *here*, my good man!"

"Simpson?" asked a rather delicate voice from behind the butler. "Did I hear someone talking about Trey?"

"I think it best that you let me deal with the situation, Miss Christina."

"If you don't mind, Simpson, I would like to know what this is about...I heard someone say there was trouble. Now if you'll just let me through..."

The butler hesitated for a couple of seconds, then begrudgingly moved a step or two to the side to reveal a girl with a fountain of blonde curls, backlit into a froth by the lights behind her; Evren knew that this must be the sister Trey had told him about.

"Hello, Miss..." Ahmet, smiling broadly, bowed slightly as he tipped his hat. "Myself I am Ahmet, I am work for Mr. Macktire, and this is Evren, the friend of Trey. Most kindly of you to see us..."

"You're Trey's driver, aren't you – what's happened to him? All Papa said was that he wasn't coming here today. Did you say there'd been some trouble?" Christina glanced at Evren as she spoke, then noticed someone else down at the bottom of the steps. Neyla quickly stepped into the shadows.

"Very much trouble, I am frightened to say, Miss." Ahmet shrugged dramatically. "Trey have somehow disappeared in a mystery circumstance."

"Trey disappeared! But how..."

"'*Mysterious circumstances*' – what's Trey got up to, Tina?" An older boy materialized at Christina's side and scrutinized Evren and Ahmet.

"I do *wish* you wouldn't call me 'Tina'. You know I hate it so…"

The boy, who, thought Evren, could only be Arthur, ignored his sister and walked out onto the wide top step. "It's fine, Simpson," he said over his shoulder. "You can leave this to me to deal with; I'll make sure they're sent on their way."

The boy sounded stern, but for some reason Evren couldn't work out he was grinning and winking at Ahmet and him as he spoke.

"Ooh, *Arthur!*" Christina's eyes widened and her lips puckered in shock. "How rude!"

Arthur turned round. "Thank you, Simpson, that will be all. I'll tell my parents about this when they return."

The butler sniffed and looked as if he'd smelled a blocked drain. "Very well, Master Arthur. If you insist…"

Arthur looked back at Evren and Ahmet and winked again. "I most certainly do…"

Except for the fact that it was pretty obvious he hadn't actually wanted to bring his sister with him, Arthur's plan – which Evren had to admit was a pretty good one – seemed to have worked perfectly. Following Arthur's instructions, Ahmet had driven his taxi round behind the house and parked out of sight. Ten minutes after the butler had been dismissed, Arthur and Christina had crept out of a side entrance and joined them in the cab; five minutes after that Arthur and Christina had been told everything that Ahmet, Evren and Neyla knew (which was not, they had to admit, very much at all).

"So, Trey saw his father throw some ruffian with a gun out of their suite, and the next thing you know his father has disappeared?" Arthur looked at Ahmet, who smiled in agreement.

"And then Trey is chased by the same people, but escapes and you," Christina butted in, pointing at Evren, "find him and take him back to *your* house –" Evren nodded – "where he discovers that his father is the dead spit of some *other* person, who's probably a spy. And then, out of the blue, *Trey* gets kidnapped and thrown into the boot of car. Have I got all that right?"

There was a moment's stunned silence in the car and everyone looked at Christina.

"A girl *can* pay attention you know, Arthur."

"I think that is completely all the story that we know, Miss Christina." Ahmet's shoulders rose and fell expressively. "Do you think your father can be the assistant in finding the Macktires?"

"I don't see how," Christina shook her head, "but we can ask."

"Well *I* think you chaps have come to *exactly* the right place! Pater is *supposed* to be the Trade Secretary here, but that's not *actually* what he does."

"What he does do?" Evren frowned.

"He runs the British Government's Military Intelligence section...he's the head of MI6's Constantinople bureau."

"Ooh, Arthur!" Christina, sitting on the back seat next to Neyla, shot forward. "You can't *possibly* know that, Arthur!"

"I jolly well can!"

"Your father is spy also?" Ahmet looked at Evren, who leaned over and muttered a quick translation to Neyla.

"In a manner of speaking," Arthur agreed.

"That is 'yes'? Or maybe is 'no'?" enquired Ahmet.

"How can you call Papa a *spy*, Arthur?"

"It's just a *name*, Tina. And everyone does it, specially here in Constantinople – I've heard Pater say spying is like a national pastime on the Continent."

"But how could you *know*?"

"Um, well... You see, I've been sort of, how shall I say, spying on *him*..."

"Oh *Arthur*, how *could* you!"

It was Arthur's turn to shrug and a hush fell inside the taxi, no one quite sure what to say next. Evren broke the awkward silence by reaching into his pocket and bringing out a sheaf of small photographic prints.

"I have picture," he said to nobody in particular.

"Who of?" asked Arthur.

"Some people." Evren flicked through the snapshots. "I have Trey's father…"

Arthur reached over and took the top print, flicking on his torch to look at it properly. "*That's* Trey's father?"

Evren shook his head. "That the man who *look* like Trey father," he held out a second print. "*This* Trey father."

Arthur took it and examined the two pictures together. "Crikey…they look like peas in a pod!"

"Is true, but my father think this one," Evren pointed to the picture of the man in the pinstripe suit, "is maybe from the Germany."

"Well I'd say your father is jolly well right!"

"How you know this thing?"

"Because I've seen him before…there was a big party at the British Consulate." Arthur gave the pictures back to Evren. "I remember, he was with the German *chargé d'affaires* and a military attaché."

"Are you making all this up, Arthur, just showing off again?" Christina looked at the others. "He shows off *all* the time, you know. Trying to prove how *awfully* clever he is."

"I do *not*! I know because I got bored at the party, and, instead of just wasting my time simpering with my silly friends, like *someone* I could mention, *I* got hold of the invitation list and went round finding out who all the guests were. And I remember *that* man, the one who looks like Trey's pater, because one of the people he was with had duelling scars on his left cheek...and they all spoke German."

"What he called?" asked Ahmet. "What he do?"

"Um...I can't remember exactly – but I kept the list, it's in a file up in my room."

"Oh *really*, Arthur..."

"Yes, really, *Tina*," Arthur opened the taxi door and jumped out. "I shall be back in a jiffy..."

20 MAKING MOVES

Trey looked round the room in the fading light. He felt a weird combination of puzzled, angry and scared and couldn't stop anxiously pacing up and down as he tried to figure out what the heck was going on. There were so *many* things he didn't know – like, was his father also in this place he'd been brought to? – that the more he thought about everything the more edgy and confused he became.

But there was one dark, distressing question in particular that kept on coming back, no matter how hard he tried to push it away. It crept up like a nasty, evil worm and it whispered to him quietly and insistently: what if, somehow, for whatever inexplicable reason, his father *was* the man in both photographs? *What then?*

He wished these stupid ideas would go away, but, now he was all alone and locked away in this small attic room in a house right on the shoreline of the Bosphorus, *somewhere* outside of Constantinople, he couldn't stop them. What if...? What if...? What if his father *had* been here before? Was it possible? Because when he thought about it, he did go away a lot and never said where. But then he'd never really asked him, had he? Trey balled his fists, gritted his teeth and shook his head – *No! No! No!* – in a concerted effort to dismiss the terrible thoughts that were eating away at him. *Why the heck would his father lie? He wouldn't! It was all baloney, a load of hooey – his father was no liar!*

Trey stopped pacing and stood still for a moment. He could put an end to this. Deep down he knew he was only thinking these crazy thoughts because he was scared, and being scared was going to get him exactly nowhere. He had to remember what Trent Gripp always said about fortune favouring the brave...he *had* to be brave, he didn't have a choice, even if it was the last thing he felt like after what he'd just been through. And one of the things that was going to help was only to think about what he *did* know, rather than all the stuff he didn't. Like the fact that the flight in the seaplane hadn't been that long, therefore it was logical to assume that he wasn't *that* far away from Constantinople.

Which was good.

But then again he didn't know how fast the plane had been flying. If he'd been in a car he might've had some chance of calculating *roughly* how far they'd travelled... he kicked the metal bed frame in sheer frustration edged with despair. He was never going to get out of this place...

Think positive, Trey, think positive! He could almost hear his gramps talking to him, almost feel him patting his back and urging him on. He'd get out of this room and this house and it wouldn't take *so* long to get back to the city. It wouldn't. Even without his trusty compass and penknife, which the pilot had found when he'd searched him, still blindfolded, before bringing him up to this room.

Thinking as confidently as he could, under the circumstances, he walked over to the door and turned the handle again, checking once more that it indeed was locked and he hadn't just been imagining it. He turned and slowly looked around at the room, examining it from top to bottom: one door and a small dormer window set into the sloping roof, and no other visible ways in or out. A couple of minutes later he was pretty sure that there were no trapdoors under the single bed or secret exits behind the wardrobe, and that (as he suspected) the window would not open.

Sitting on the bed, its thin mattress sagging and the sprung steel mesh it lay on creaking like a set of unoiled hinges, Trey took stock of his situation. So what else did he know for sure? He glanced out at the sky and then at his watch, which thankfully seemed to have survived the manhandling he'd had well enough; it was almost 8.00 p.m., and dusk was beginning to fall outside. Trey got up and went to the window where he saw the last of the sun casting great elongated shadows across the waters lapping the front of the house. Okay, so now he *also* knew that he was on the western side of the Bosphorus, which he remembered ran vaguely north/south. And that meant, even without his compass, he was sure Constantinople was somewhere to his right. Useful information if – *when* – he got out of the house.

Trey was standing so close to the glass that his breath misted, so he took a step back...and noticed that the reason the window wouldn't open was that it had basically been *painted* shut, and that more than likely all he really needed to get it open again was a penknife. Which, of course, he didn't actually *have* with him any more. As he cursed his bad luck his stomach growled back at him, a reminder that he hadn't eaten a thing since the sesame breadsticks he'd bought in the market.

As if in answer to his silent wish for food Trey heard the rattle of a key in a lock. Not wanting to be caught looking out of the window, as if whoever came into the room would somehow know he was thinking of ways to escape, he quickly sat back down on the bed and waited. When the door finally opened it revealed a young square-jawed, blond-haired man almost standing to attention as he held a tray in his left hand.

"*Bleib dort* – stay!" he grunted, frowning.

"Okay..." Trey did as he was told and stayed exactly where he was. This person was someone new, another German he'd not seen before, and he wondered who else was in the house. Just the two of them? And maybe his father?

"For you to eat." The young man bent down and put the tray on the floor, pushing it into the room before closing the door and firmly relocking it.

Trey went over and took a look at what had been left for him, much like you'd leave food for a dog: a plate of food – an unappetizingly grey piece of meat, a few pale over-boiled vegetables, a slice of bread, a mug of water...and a knife and fork. A bone-handled knife with a serrated blade. Just the thing for attempting to open a window that had been painted shut. Which he would set about doing just as soon as he'd eaten the food...

"I really must apologize for my brother's behaviour, he honestly really is the *most* terrible show-off...the limit, really," Christina announced, a few minutes after Arthur had exited the taxi, leaving everyone a little flummoxed. "But I'm *very* glad you all came as we really *must* find a way to help poor Trey and his father."

"Yes..." said Ahmet from the front of the car, where he sat, tapping the steering wheel with his thumbs. "But how?"

"I suppose we shall just have to wait and see if Arthur really *does* have a file with anything in it..." Christina's tone of voice made it obvious that she didn't think it especially likely.

"And if he does not?" Evren asked as Neyla whispered something in his ear and Ahmet turned round and looked over into the back of the taxi.

"What's she saying?"

"Neyla ask when your father and mother they come back."

"Late, why?"

Before anyone could answer Christina's question the front passenger door opened and everyone jumped as Arthur appeared out of nowhere and got in next to Ahmet; he had a number of buff-coloured foolscap folders tucked under one arm and was looking extremely pleased with himself.

"Very quick jiffy!" Evren said.

"I should say so – I'm in the 100 yard sprint team at school!"

"What you have there with you?"

"Valuable information!" Arthur grinned, switching on his torch and opening the top folder with a flourish. "The man who looks like Trey's pater is a German called Reinhardt Gessler, and my investigations at the party showed that he works for the *Abwehr*."

"*Investigations...*" huffed Christina. "And whatever are the *Abwehr* when they're at home?"

"The German intelligence service, actually, Tina. So there."

"He is spy, also?" Evren leaned over between the seats to look at the open folder on Arthur's lap.

"Looks like it, chum."

"What is in the other that you have?"

"The other files?" Arthur opened the second folder in the pile. "This is a group photograph – you know, everyone who was at the party at the Consulate? They always have one taken."

Ahmet reached over and, much to Arthur's surprise,

took the photo and torch out of his hands, examining the large black and white print extremely closely. "I know this man," he said at last, indicating a man standing, half-hidden, at the back of the photograph; he gave the torch and picture back to Arthur. "This is a Russia man. He is absolutely one of them who has been following Mr. Macktire."

"Really? Let me just check who he is…" Arthur ran his finger down a list of names. "He's called Stanislaus Levedski – but how'd *you* know he was Russian?"

"They are not the only one who can make the follow," Ahmet said, proudly patting his chest. "I go behind the man, without him knowing, and see where in the end he stops."

"And where was that?" asked Arthur.

"A house."

"A house? Do you mean the Russian Consulate, Ahmet?"

"No, but not so far from it. I make secret enquiries from someone and they tell me all who live there are Russia people."

"But why would the *Russians* want to kidnap Trey, Arthur?" asked Christina.

"I think maybe they are the people who take his father also," said Evren. "Maybe they think they have Herr Reinhardt Gessler. My father say that Rusya and

Almanya – the Russia and Germany – don't one agree with the other. This could be the reason, maybe?"

"D'you know," exclaimed Arthur, "I think you might have something there, old chap! These upstart Soviet types have been acting like pirates recently, and things aren't so chipper in Germany right now…I've read about it in Pater's newspaper."

"Are you going to tell Papa, when he and Mama come back, so he can get them released?"

"No."

"No? But why not?" Christina rolled her eyes. "Oh *Arthur*…you haven't got another one of your silly ideas up your sleeve have you?"

"It is *not* a silly idea, Tina. It's one of my very best."

"But…"

"You know Pater isn't going to listen to me, not after the last time. So, if this job's going to be done, it's going to *have* to be done by us!"

"Excuse," Ahmet butted in, "but what you have up your sleeves?"

"It's a bit complicated, old chap…"

"It's not, Arthur, it's quite simple, really." Everyone turned to look at Christina, who, this time, didn't seem to mind. "My papa thinks Arthur is a bit of a fibber, you see."

"Fibber?" queried Evren.

"He makes up stories," explained Christina. "And so Arthur thinks Papa won't believe it when he tells him that Trey and his father are being held captive by the Russians."

"It's the Soviets, and I *didn't* make up the story about the chap from Serbia...he *was* a bounder, he just didn't have a *bomb*!"

"A bomb?" Ahmet's eyebrows shot up.

"Can it be possible to tell this so that we," Evren indicated himself, Neyla and Ahmet, "should know what you are saying?"

"The truth is, Tina – *Christina* – is right; my pater probably *wouldn't* believe me if I told him what we think has happened to Trey and his father. So my idea is that *we* all go to the house where the Russians are and get them out—"

"But we don't know that's where they've been taken, do we, Arthur?"

Arthur looked at his sister through slitted eyes. "Well we *won't* know unless we go and take a look, will we?"

Christina smiled sweetly. "I just thought that should be clear."

"Right..." Arthur took a deep breath. "So, later on tonight, when everyone else has gone to bed, *we* go to the house Ahmet found...what d'you chaps say?"

"What do you think?" Evren spoke to Ahmet and

Neyla in Turkish. "No one is going to believe *us* either if we tell them."

"Not even Baba Duan?" asked Neyla.

"My baba would believe us, but who would believe *him*?"

"But Baba Duan is a good man!"

"True, but he always tells me that, because he's a journalist, people believe his job is to tell lies for money, which he says is only true sometimes." Evren glanced at Arthur and Christina, who were both listening intently, but not understanding a word of what was being said. "What should we do, Ahmet?"

"I think we must try to at least see if they are in the Russians' house." Ahmet rubbed his chin as he thought everything over. "And *if* we find them, we can make another plan to get them out."

"Do I need to tell him?" Evren nodded sideways at Arthur.

"He is clever," mused Ahmet.

"And he is English, from a rich family," said Neyla. "If we get into trouble, he could pay to get us out of it."

Ahmet's face broke into a wide grin and he snorted with laughter.

"What's so funny?" Arthur frowned. "What have you been talking about?"

"Just discuss," said Evren. "We will meet you, where

we are now, at two hours in the night-time – is that good, Ahmet?"

Ahmet nodded.

"I'll be here." Arthur gathered his papers together. "Two o'clock on the dot!"

"Why for you do this?"

Arthur's hand stopped halfway to the car door and frowned at Evren. "What d'you mean?"

"You are not such big friends with Trey, I think."

"We like him," said Christina. "At least I do."

"That's not *really* the point... Look, when a chap's in trouble, well, you have to do the right thing, don't you?" Arthur got out of the car, then turned back round and poked his head back inside. "And of course, it'll also be a *beezer* wheeze!"

21 UPS AND DOWNS

Scraping layers of paint off parts of a sash window – even a relatively small sash window – turned out to be no easy job, especially when all you had to do it with was a fairly blunt knife, and a fork. But, Trey reminded himself as he quietly chipped away flake after flake, a fairly blunt knife (and a fork) was so much better than having nothing at all to do the job with.

It was now completely dark outside – and inside the room, as there was no light – and all he could do was mentally keep his fingers crossed that the blond man would *not* come back upstairs to take away his plate, instead leaving the job till morning. By when, if his luck held, he'd be miles away.

Think positive!

Trey had been hard at work for well over an hour and his hands were aching, fingers getting raw and tender, but at least he was getting results for all his efforts: the fork had proved to be a pretty useless tool, but he was now able to get the knife blade in down both sides of the window and almost all the way along the top edge. Once he'd managed to clear that there would only be the bottom to go.

Which was when the blade got stuck, and broke as he tried to get it out...

He stood, staring at the handle (which now sported an inch and a bit of snapped metal where a moment before there had been *five* inches of stainless steel) and wanted to kick something good and hard. What the triple darn was he going to do now? And then Trey noticed, as the moonlight glinted off it, that the broken edge was in fact much sharper than the original blade had probably ever been. Just as his gramps liked to say: it was a heck of an ill wind that didn't blow *someone* some good!

A few more minutes of feverish activity and the paint was hacked and scraped off on all four sides of the sash window. Trey took a deep breath and shoved upwards.

Nothing.

He shoved again, harder this time, but all that happened was that the window moved a fraction of an inch and the broken part of the blade got dislodged, making something of a racket as it fell onto the outside ledge below. Trey waited to see if the noise had alerted anyone to what he was up to, but as the seconds ticked by he reckoned he'd gotten away with it. He was, though, still left facing the fact that the window stubbornly continued refusing to budge. What he needed now was a can of 3-in-One oil, which again, like the penknife, he had...except it was in the utility room in Chicago, up on the shelf above his trusty bike.

And then a light bulb clicked on in his head.

Trey went over and got the plate, which still had what was left over from his meal on it: the rather olly gravy that he hadn't even bothered to wipe up with his bread because it was so disgustingly greasy. He looked at the small pool of brownish liquid and shrugged...it was all he had, and he was grateful for it, but if this didn't work he was going to be up a gum tree, and no mistake about it.

Picking up the plate he took it over to the window and, as carefully as he could, dripped vaguely equal amounts of the gravy onto each side of the window. Working what was left over into any crack he could find,

Trey then wiped his hands as clean as he could on the bed sheet. This was going to be it. Now or never.

Cracking his knuckles, Trey squared his shoulders and went back to the window. Taking a deep breath he shoved upwards as hard as he could, and to his utter amazement (and no little relief), little by little the sash began to move. Four or so inches up it stuck, but he didn't panic or lose hope. He could see that this was quite enough space for him to get his arm through and use his shoulder to heave and strain, which he did. He pushed and pushed and pushed until the gap was about a foot wide. And then he stopped, his shoulder hurting like billy-o and sweat pouring off him like he'd been out in the rain.

Right, he thought to himself, let's get out of here!

Trey stood for a moment, getting his breath back, then he poked his head through the gap and for the first time took in quite how steep the pitch of the roof was. Added to which the attic was three storeys up from the water's edge – he'd made a point of counting how many landings there were as he'd been none too gently pushed up the stairs to the room he was now in.

Back inside the room, it didn't take long for him to figure out that there were but two options available to him. He could try and slide down to the edge of the roof, find a drainpipe (did they even *have* drainpipes on houses in this neck of the woods?) and attempt to get down without falling or being heard. Or...and here Trey's palms got all sweaty...or he could dive off the roof into the water below. Or jump. Would jumping be better?

In the end it was the fact that hitting the water would be far less likely to do him permanent damage than hitting solid ground that decided matters. He would dive. And, as it was midnight, he should get his skates on and make his move.

Preparations did not take long. Trey recalled a story called *The Dangerous Miss Daniels* in a recent issue of *Black Ace* where the gumshoe hero had escaped certain death by diving from a small boat about to go over a waterfall and into the pool some hundred and fifty feet below. All he'd done was take his socks and size 10 brown shoes off and tie them to his belt, also tying his jacket round his waist, the theory being that this would make swimming easier. Whether the writer had actually tried this out before putting the idea in his story, Trey hadn't a clue, but all he could do was hope and pray that he hadn't simply made it up to get him – and his hero – out of a tight spot.

Just as he was about to climb out of the window, shoes and jacket attached as per the story, something occurred to Trey...to buy himself a bit more time, he should make some kind of shape in the bed so if the man *did* come and collect the tray he might assume that his captive was asleep and all was well with the world. Grabbing the spare pillow and blanket he knew from his previous search were in the wardrobe, Trey quickly constructed a rough "body" shape on the mattress and covered it; standing back to admire his handiwork the muffled sound of footsteps on uncarpeted wooden stairs brought him back down to earth with a bang – he was going to be well and truly caught red-handed if the man came to get the tray now!

He was still frozen to the spot when he heard a door somewhere below open and close. No more footsteps. Letting out a huge sigh, and wondering just how much more of this his nerves could take, Trey went back to the window and eased his way out onto the ledge, pulling the curtains across and then pushing the sash down behind him, as leaving them open would be a real giveaway.

Trey's hands and bare feet sought and found purchase on the rough wooden shingles and he gingerly left the comparative safety of the window ledge, inching his way forward. Slowly. Very, *very* slowly. Trying not to make any noise that would sound like someone attempting to get down a roof, the ten or twelve feet took Trey what seemed like hours; the clammy sweat he was working up dried in the cool night air, making him shiver, until finally he was at the jump-off-or-dive point.

It was a long, long way down.

Could he do it?

He had to.

There was no going back.

Except...what if the water *did* turn out to be too shallow?

It wouldn't be too shallow, it would be *fine*.

It just would be...

Trey gingerly leaned forward, trying desperately to keep his balance. He was only going to have one chance to do this, no second go-round if he didn't *quite* get it right first time. A cloud scudded across the three-quarter moon, and in the darker dark he could see that there were no other lights from the house shining on the water: hopefully that meant everyone was asleep. For the first time he looked left and right, but found there was nothing to see.

He glanced at his watch: twenty-five to one... his watch! It was *not* going to survive this experience, but there was nothing he could do about it. As long as *he* did, that was all that counted – which was maybe what he should start doing. He should count himself down to the dive. It might help.

One...he sat back on his heels.

Two...he took a deep breath.

Three...he checked his shoes and jacket were tied tight.

Trey sat down again, shaking his head and *hating* himself for being such a wimp. If he carried on like this, *this* is where they'd find him, come morning, and he would have failed. If he was going to have *any* chance of finding his father he *had* to get off this roof, and sitting, loafing about on it was not going to help matters one iota, jot or tittle, as Gramps liked to say.

It was the realization of what his gramps would think if he knew how he was carrying on that did it. No more countdowns, no more deep breaths and last-minute checks! He had a job to do! Mr. Charles Lindbergh would *never* have made it solo across the Atlantic if he'd thought about it too much, and Major Bernardi wouldn't have won the Schneider Trophy if he'd had to keep on taking deep breaths!

Trey stood up, put his hands out in front of him, braced his legs and, like Trent Gripp, he went for it...

22 INS AND OUTS

Evren peeked out of the shadows to look up and down the street. Empty, except for a couple of cats marking their territory, which was exactly how it should have been at sometime after two o'clock in the morning. He disappeared back out of sight.

"Well?" enquired Arthur slightly nervously. This was not only far and away the latest he'd ever been up, it was also *the* most exciting thing he'd *ever* done! He glanced at Neyla, face smeared with dirt like him and Evren, and thought about Christina, back at the house and tucked up fast asleep; how different the two girls were. He could not imagine his sister hiding in a back alley and about to embark on some serious espionage, reconnaissance and undercover work. She would have stuck out like the proverbial sore thumb, not to mention that she didn't even *own* a pair of dark long trousers!

"Is fine. We can go." Evren glanced at Neyla and winked.

Arthur readied himself to go. "What about Mr. Ahmet, what's he going to be doing?"

"He sleep."

"Sleep?"

"Yes." Evren indicated back down the street with his thumb. "In his taxi car, where he stay for us. This not a job for him. He is good at waiting and driving, not climbing walls and running."

"Running? You mean as in being chased?"

"It could maybe happen."

"Oh...right..." Arthur was very glad to know that, if there should be any chasing, there was at least a car they could jump in for a quick getaway. "By the way, who's paying Mr. Ahmet for all the waiting and driving?"

"Mr. Macktire," said Evren, doing a final check of the two sacks he and Neyla had with them, one of which squeaked disconcertingly when he touched it.

"Trey's *father* – how?"

"He pay Ahmet for a whole week of days, and as he has not driven too much, he say he can do some of the night, too."

"Decent of him."

Evren didn't answer, instead he stood and picked up the squeaking sack. "You go with Neyla," he said, then slid away.

"Come." Neyla beckoned, picking up the other, smaller sack and making off in the opposite direction.

"Right-*oh!*" said Arthur, following her.

Arthur was a dead shot with a catapult. Years of practice dispatching tin cans and bottles at the bottom of the garden meant that firing stones at something as large as a *window* was like falling off a log. And his latest catty, which was undoubtedly the very best he'd ever made, was a demon. He pulled the elastic back as far as he could and let rip, sending a conker-sized stone right to the centre of his target. The ground floor window in the house Ahmet had pinpointed as the one he'd seen the Russian going into smashed into smithereens quite impressively. Now he was sure of his range, Arthur's next three shots all hit their targets as well, as did Neyla's rather less elegantly thrown missiles.

If you'd been watching you might have noticed a

shadowy figure appear outside one of the broken windows and shove something through the jagged hole before disappearing. Neyla and Arthur, who *were* watching, almost missed Evren playing his part in their plan to find Trey and his father – which was to release a sackful of rats inside the house.

Abandoning their small sack of rocks and stones, Arthur and Neyla ran across the street to join Evren, and waited. What was *supposed* to happen next was that the surprise "attack" and subsequent rat invasion would create enough panic to allow them to sneak into the house and, in the turmoil and uproar, take a look around. And it had, not so long ago in the back of Ahmet's taxi, seemed like a terrific idea.

Which, but for two quite unforeseen things, it was.

As the expected confusion broke out, instead of the occupants stumbling round in total darkness, there was a blaze of light from inside the house, as it turned out to be – just their luck – one of the few houses in Constantinople with electricity. And then the shouts of panic, anger and surprise were joined by gunfire as random pistol shots rang out.

"We can't go in there!" Arthur grabbed Evren's arm. "We should get back to the car, now!"

"We could maybe see what happens," Evren said, "from across the street?"

Before Arthur could stop him, Evren, followed by Neyla, was sprinting back across the road and there was nothing else he could do but follow them. The curtains weren't drawn in the downstairs rooms and peering round the corner of a house opposite they watched the mayhem as the rats, which Evren had personally collected, continued to create havoc. They saw a couple of irate men in pyjamas jumping around waving pistols (and another running here and there wielding a broom), attempting to clear the house of its sudden, inexplicable infestation of rocks and vermin. Lights were on in the upstairs rooms as well, a man poking his head out of one of the windows, probably trying to see who might have been responsible for the stone throwing.

But, as far as any of them could see, there was no sign of Trey or his father; although this was obviously quite a disappointment, something about the scene reminded Arthur of the high jinks in a Christmas panto he and Christina had been taken to back in London. Even though the men in the house were actually firing real bullets – and, if they'd gone inside, would no doubt have been firing at them – he couldn't stop himself from giggling.

"This was not so good idea," muttered Evren, not at all amused by what had happened.

"It *seemed* like a good idea, old chap; on paper,

at least..." Arthur said, a noise behind him making him glance over his shoulder as he spoke; he saw that windows were being opened and people looking out to see what all the palaver and commotion was about. This did seem as if it would be an opportune moment to make good their escape. *"Time to go!"* he whispered hoarsely into Evren's ear, and took off down the street.

The wrong way.

Arthur only realized his mistake when he heard his name being called and turned to see Neyla beckoning for him to follow her, and then high-tailing it after Evren in the opposite direction. As he ran Arthur heard voices shouting and footsteps clattering – he'd been seen! They were going to try and catch him!

Imagining he was on the sports field at school and taking part in the most important 440 yard race of his entire life, Arthur powered forward. Sprinting as if his life depended on it (because, if he was caught, and his father *ever* found out what he'd been up to, his life would *not* be worth living) he ran like he'd never run before, quickly catching up with Neyla and then easily overtaking both her and Evren. Slowing a bit as he skidded round a corner, arms flailing wildly in an effort to keep his balance, Arthur picked up speed again and almost ran straight past Ahmet's taxi. Sliding to a halt he grabbed a handle, yanked a door open and tumbled onto the floor at the back of the car, nearly giving Ahmet, who was still fast asleep, a heart attack.

"Step on the gas!" Arthur yelled breathlessly as he got up, only to be knocked down again by Neyla diving into the back with him.

"What?" spluttered Ahmet. "What happen?"

Evren rattled off something in Turkish, Ahmet slapped his forehead with his palm and immediately turned the engine over. The starter motor wheezed like a creature about to die.

"I say, chaps..." said Arthur, who had risked a quick look out of the back window and seen someone – someone who looked like they *could* be carrying a pistol – running their way. "Could we get a move on?"

At that moment the engine caught and rumbled into life with a loud backfire. As Ahmet engaged first gear and accelerated away there was an answering couple of bangs as the man who had been following them, thinking he was under attack, returned fire at the car.

23 A LONG WAY TO GO

It was a terrifically long way down, or at least it seemed that way to Trey, diving towards the coal black waters of the Bosphorus. As he flew like an arrow, the cold night air singing in his ears, he tried to keep in mind what he'd been taught at his swimming lessons...*keep your head down; keep your arms completely straight in front, hands together, like a knife to cut the water; don't let your legs wave about and keep your feet as parallel to your legs as you can.* All of which wouldn't matter one tiny bit if the water was too shallow, of course.

Before he'd launched himself off the roof, Trey had taken one last deep breath, which he had held all the way down. The shock of hitting the water made him breathe out, which was exactly the right thing to do as he plunged down, the drag from his clothes and the shoes tied to his belt slowing him up; and then he remembered, too late, that he should have pushed his hands up the moment after he hit the water so that he wouldn't go too deep. Trey bent backwards, pushing at the water with his arms and kicking as powerfully as he could; opening his eyes he could see there was light above him, although he couldn't tell how far away it was, and he swam towards it for all he was worth. Now that he hadn't crowned himself by diving into water that wasn't deep enough, he didn't want to end up drowning because he'd gone down too far.

Five seconds later – five of what had to be the *longest* seconds in the entire *history* of the whole world, in his opinion – Trey broke the surface, completely disoriented and sucking in air like there was no tomorrow. He trod water for a moment or two, swinging round left and right until he'd finally got his bearings.

He floated low in the water, his clothes clinging to him like folds of sagging skin, shoes still attached to his belt and, amazingly, his jacket still tied round his waist, and he looked up at the house. It wasn't built at the water's edge, as he'd assumed, but right *over* the water, with twin boat houses under the veranda. As far as he could tell his dive hadn't prompted anybody to turn a lamp on and look out of a window to see what had happened. Yet.

Still and all, hanging around in the water, right in front of the house where anyone who *did* take a look might spot him, was probably not a terrific idea. Best that he got himself to shore as quick as he could so he could decide what to do next – attempt to get back *into* the house to see if his father was there, or start making his way back to Constantinople for help.

It took seconds to figure that getting help was his only real option as he did *not* want to get caught. Remembering that south was to his left, Trey started swimming, breaststroking as quietly as possible in that direction, figuring that he'd better get further away from the house before he made for the shore. Which was when he saw the seaplane.

Bobbing on its floats, with its double set of wings making it look kind of old-fashioned in comparison to Major Bernardi's sleek, red, single-winged Macchi M.52, the plane was moored downriver from the house; as Trey swam towards it he allowed himself to imagine that in fact he *was* an experienced pilot. That the Italians had taught him *everything* he needed to know back in

Venice and all he had to do was climb up into the cockpit, turn the engine over, and before the men who had kidnapped him knew anything about it he'd be airborne! The truth of the matter was he had absolutely *no* idea how to fly the seaplane, but it did occur to him that something useful might've been left in it – like, maybe, a map?

You never knew.

Trey glided over to the nearest float and used one of the struts to help pull himself up onto it, his waterlogged clothing doing its level best to pull him into the water again. The plane rocked back and forth as he stood up rather unsteadily. Holding onto the lower wing, with water cascading off him, the night air suddenly made him shiver quite violently, his chattering teeth sounding like someone was playing a game of pick-up with knucklebones *inside* his head. Moving along the float he ducked under the wing, coming up below the pilot's cockpit.

Carefully hauling himself up onto the lower wing he took a look and saw nothing there that seemed like it was going to be any use to him. He was about to look in the rear cockpit, where the co-pilot would sit, when it occurred to him that this must've been where they'd dumped the case with him in it! Incensed at the treatment he'd had, Trey reached into the cockpit and grabbed a lever at random...then he stopped for a moment, feeling just a *bit* guilty that he was about to vandalize a beautiful machine. Only for a moment, though, and only a *very* tiny bit guilty: these were bad people. Then he yanked sideways on the lever as hard as he could and it came off in his hand.

Try flying without *that*, he thought as he held on tight and leaned over at a fairly perilous angle to see whether there might be anything of interest in the back. Peering into the dark space Trey saw, tantalizingly just out of reach, the shape of what looked like it could possibly be a leather briefcase on the seat. But if he was going to get his hands on it he was somehow going to have to get an awful lot nearer. "Nothing ventured, nothing gained", that's what good old Pistol Gripp would say, so he ventured, clinging to the side of the cockpit, legs dangling down, and scrambling with his bare feet until he eventually fell head first onto the seat.

Squirming himself back upright, Trey got a hold of what he'd seen on the seat and discovered that it was, after all, a rather excellent brown leather case, like a very grown up satchel, complete with brass clasps, a handle and a shoulder strap. It was pretty heavy, like all the best presents on your birthday or at Christmas were, and feeling quite excited he undid it and took a peek inside. Papers. And a gun. An automatic pistol, by the look of it.

Trey could feel his pulse racing. A gun. He had a gun! Just like Trent and all the sleuths in the *Black Ace* stories. It was kind of careless of the people who'd grabbed him to leave it out here on the plane, but, he supposed, this did seem like it was the boondocks. And who would expect a kid to jump off the top of the roof in the middle of the night?

He was just about to start the process of getting himself out of the cockpit and back down onto the float when he heard a noise. His nerves completely on edge, Trey immediately sank down in the seat. Was someone out there? Did they have a guard, patrolling round the house? How the *heck* was he going to get ashore now? Panic spread like blood from a gunshot wound, the dread of being found and taken back to that attic room making his scalp tighten. Hunkered down out of sight Trey then cottoned on that what he was hearing wasn't footsteps at all, and that now he could also hear some kind of snuffling.

Snuffling?

He inched his way upwards until, in the gloom, he saw it. A pig. And not the kind of jolly *Piggly Wiggly*-style porker like you might expect to see on a farm, but a big old wild boar. On its way to who knew where, the stocky, bristle-covered animal took a last look around and then trotted off, disappearing into the night. Trey sat up. It dawned on him that, wherever he was, the fact there were wild boar out there meant it was proper countryside. With who knew what other wild animals. He looked at the briefcase he was hugging, in which there was a gun. Trey glanced over at the shoreline and let out a sigh…all he had to do now was somehow find a way of swimming over to it *without* getting the pistol wet and everything would be just fine and dandy.

A quick search of the cockpit of the seaplane showed that it was entirely devoid of anything waterproof to wrap the briefcase in (the search did, however, throw up a couple of maps – the reason he'd taken a look in the plane in the first place – which he stuffed in the briefcase without looking at them), so he'd just have to find another way.

Trey carefully slid down onto the float nearest to the shore and lay the briefcase on the float; easing himself back into the cold, black water he looked behind to gauge how far he had to go and took a deep breath – which was nowhere near as meaningful as the one he'd taken on the edge of the rooftop. Reaching up for the briefcase, he held it as high as possible over his head and struck out, kicking as hard as he could.

It wasn't *that* far to the shore, but it felt like he was *never* going to get there. His shoulders were aching, he was getting more and more tired (and the case getting nearer and nearer to the water) with every kick, *and* he was making what sounded like an unholy racket as well. Then his foot hit gravel and mud. Trey splashed to a halt and stumbled to his feet knowing exactly how a drowning rat must feel. And look.

Holding the briefcase out to the side so he didn't dribble water onto it, Trey dragged himself up to the top of the slope and sank to the ground, shaking the Bosphorus out of his hair. He'd made it. And *all* he had to do now was make it to Constantinople... He looked to his left at the silhouette of the house. Even if his father *was* being held a prisoner there, no matter which way he looked at it, the only way forward was to find help. If his father was there, he had to leave him. And if he *wasn't* there, Trey had to find him.

He unknotted his jacket from around his waist and wrung as much of the water out of it as he could, laying it on the ground beside him, then took his balled-up socks (which contained his wristwatch) out of one of his shoes. The lame attempt to stop his watch from getting too wet had failed miserably and it was now stuck at just after half past twelve. For ever. Trey put it on anyway and tried to undo the laces attaching his shoes to his belt. It was no easy job as his fingers were numb, waterlogged and wrinkly, while the laces had swollen and at first refused to budge.

Finally, as damp, uncomfortable and tired as he felt, he was at last ready to go, and then he remembered the maps. He got them out and discovered, by the light of the silvery moon (the tune, one of his mother's favourites, started to run in his head) that they were German, which he might know the sound of but he couldn't read. One of the maps had *Das Königreich von Serben, von Kroaten und von Slovenes* on the cover, which even he could tell was going to be no help at all to him, but the other map was titled *Die Türkei: Konstantinopolis und das Bosphorus*. Trey opened it up to find that it was going to be a lot more useful than he could ever have imagined.

Someone had helpfully marked on it what Trey took to be a rough flight path, with what looked like compass bearings and other notations every so often. The pencil line went from Constantinople (or Konstantinopolis) to where he could make out that the word *haus* had been neatly written next to a dot on the western side of the Bosphorus.

There was nothing else marked on the map. No sign of a town or a village, or houses, for that matter. This really was Nowheresville, good and proper.

But, while Trey couldn't fly himself back he could read a map, and he was sure, if he kept close to the line he figured must be a road, that he'd find his way okay.

He'd bet good money on it (if he was allowed to). Refolding the map he stashed it in the briefcase, which he slung over his shoulder, and wearily stood up. "Time to move on out," he muttered to himself, like ranch-hands in the Saturday morning Tom Mix movies always did. "Git along there…"

24 IRONS IN THE FIRE

Baba Duan had not let grass grow under his feet since Herr Reinhardt Gessler's visit. In fact, much like his eldest son, he too had been busy; going here, there and everywhere else, he'd worked until the early hours doing what he did best: gathering information. His methods, unlike Evren's, were much more subtle and they had, also unlike Evren's, been really quite successful.

Circumstances had seen to it that father and son had absolutely no idea what the other had been up to. Baba

Duan had already left the house when Evren came rushing back to tell him what had happened to Trey, and he didn't come home until some thirty minutes *after* Ahmet had dropped Evren off. Thinking that his father was at home, and still a little shaken that they'd been shot at by the Russians, Evren had sneaked back into the house, silent as a moth. He'd gone straight to bed and not heard his father come home.

Even though Baba Duan had only managed a few hours' sleep, he was up (as he knew the English liked to say) with the lark. Although, to be honest, he could not remember the last time he'd seen one of those birds in Constantinople. He had a plan, and as anyone with any sense at all knew, a plan would remain nothing but hot air, speculation and guesswork until it was put into practice. Whistling to himself, Baba Duan strolled into the kitchen, patting his recently-shaved cheeks, to find Evren already at the table and involved with a bowl of figs, a slab of bread and a glass of tea.

"Ah...well, well," Baba Duan looked slightly taken aback at finding someone else, albeit his adored first-born, in the kitchen. "Another early bird. Is it because of some job that I've forgotten I have given you, or are you maybe going to see Trey?"

"Um, no, Baba..." Evren had been hoping to get out of the house without seeing anyone, so he didn't have to answer any awkward questions…like where had he been when there was work to be done (there was *always* work to be done), and what time had he *eventually* got back? But now that his father was standing there in front of him he knew he'd better come clean about everything. "I cannot see Trey, Baba."

"Oh? Why not?"

"I don't know where he is."

"At the Consulate, surely…no?"

"No, Baba." Evren shook his head. He sat back in his chair, his appetite gone, and began telling his father what had happened the day before. He gave every detail that he could remember of the events, like his father had taught him a good reporter should be able to do. When he'd finished, Baba Duan had also finished the figs, bread and cup of tea.

"You did well, Evren, very well. Although what might have happened if you had really gone in the house and been caught I do not know. Did the Russians *really* shoot at you?"

Evren nodded. "But only because the car backfired. I think." He got up and went to get some more food, his appetite having returned, now that he'd told the whole story and his father hadn't bitten his head off. "What can we do now, Baba? The same men who have his father have got Trey as well."

"We don't know that..."

While his son had told him *his* side of the story, chapter and verse, Baba Duan didn't think it appropriate that he was as honest in return. When it came to information, he believed, not *everybody* needed to know absolutely *everything*. "Even after your adventure with Neyla and the English boy," Baba Duan continued, "we still don't know exactly who it is who has either of them. That is still a mystery which remains to be solved."

"But *how*, Baba?"

"Let me put it this way," Baba Duan took some more of the food his son had brought to the table, "I have some irons in the fire. Which is, in the present state of this and that, the best I can be doing at the minute."

Evren knew his father well enough to know that he had not been telling him the whole story. Baba Duan had a way of licking his lips when there was more to tell than he was prepared to say. Or when he was being less than truthful. He remembered the first time he'd realized that Baba Duan was lying to him. It had been a shock to find out that his trusted parent could do that, and he'd angrily confronted his father, demanding to know why he'd done it. "We should both treat this as a lesson," Baba Duan had replied, seemingly not at all put out that he'd been caught. "A wise man once said 'Any fool can tell the truth, but it takes a shrewd and clever one to lie well', and I believe he was right; I was found out because I was careless, and you were cleverer than I gave you credit for."

Evren heard the front door close downstairs and leaned out of the kitchen window just in time to see his father turn the corner and disappear. Evren still found it odd that he was wearing a bowler hat, instead of his beloved red fez, but, for some inexplicable reason, the government had banned the wearing of fezzes the previous year (on pain of death...he *really* didn't understand that). Part of him wanted to drop everything and follow his father to see where he was going, but a sensible voice reminded him that he'd made an agreement with Neyla to meet early and then go on up to Arthur's house.

The night before Ahmet had apologized for not being able to join them, because, he'd said, he had a family to feed and had to get back to work. So, whatever they decided to do next, they were going to have to do it without the aid of a car and driver. Which Evren was all too aware was going to severely limit any course of action they might come up with.

* * *

Arthur and his sister were barely on speaking terms. Christina could not *believe* that her brother had gone out with the others and left her behind! And she particularly didn't like his claim that when he'd left she'd been snoring. The absolute truth was that he'd sneaked out and left her behind on purpose because he *never* liked to take her *any*where with him. And the only reason she was saying anything at all to him was because she knew that the perfectly *rotten* boy would quite prefer it if she actually *didn't* say anything.

Somewhere outside a dog barked twice. Christina noticed her brother look up from his desk, where he was sitting squirting oil onto parts of one of his silly trains. She saw him stop what he was doing and listen, his frown turning to a smile when the dog then barked three more times, and then twice again. Out of the corner of her eye she watched him put the green liveried train and red oil can down, absent-mindedly wiping his hands on his trousers (if Miss Renyard had caught him doing *that* he'd have been in trouble!) and make for the playroom door.

Christina beat him to it and stood, blocking his way. "Where are you going?"

"Mind your own beeswax." Arthur attempted to dodge round his sister. "Nosey parker."

"I am *not*!"

"*Are!*"

"*Not!*"

Outside the dog barked again, in exactly the same way, and Arthur's face took on an extremely agitated expression.

"That isn't a dog, is it?" Christina smiled in a way she knew would *really* annoy her brother, and was pleased to see that it did. "It's Evren and Neyla, isn't it, Arthur?" Arthur looked like he'd just swallowed a spoonful of particularly vile cough mixture. "If you don't let me come with you I shall tell. Just you see if I don't."

"But that's *black*mail!"

"I know." Christina opened the door. "Shall we go?"

Baba Duan tipped his hat and smiled at the gardener as he walked up to the building and rapped on the front door of the British Consulate. He was eyeing up his reflection in the glass and thinking that, even though the bowler hat was undoubtedly smart, he would still prefer to wear a fez, when the door opened. A young man in a suit that appeared to be rather too tight for him (and who definitely looked like he should sharpen his razor before he used it again) stood looking at him questioningly.

"Yes?"

"Mister, the Honourable George Archibald Stanhope-Leigh, His Majesty's servant and Trade Secretary."

"Excuse me?'

"I should very much like to have the distinct pleasure of a meeting. With him."

"Really..." The junior assistant secretary looked at the large, obviously Turkish man, dressed in a pin-striped suit and wearing a bowler hat, and frowned. "And you would be?"

"I would be the Mister Duan Hendek, journalistic reporter of foreign correspondence for several various international newspapers of much repute..." Baba Duan dug two fingers into one of his waistcoat pockets. "My card!"

"Ah...thank you..." The young man was just about to take the small piece of off-white pasteboard when it was summarily whisked away from him.

"Apologies!" Baba Duan smiled broadly as he drew out another card (one that actually had "Duan Hendek" printed on it, rather than one of his alternative identities), and handed it over. "This one, somehow *nicer*."

"Mister..." the junior assistant secretary glanced curiously at the card, "...Hendek. Well, I'm afraid you will need an appointment if you want to see the Trade Secretary, and I'm sorry to say that his diary is *rather* crowded at the moment. It *is* possible he might have some time available next week – would you like me to check?"

"Excuse me." Baba Duan reached out and plucked the card out of the young man's hand; taking a small, stainless steel propelling pencil from the breast pocket of his jacket he wrote something on the blank reverse side and handed it back again. "Give this to the Honourable Mr. Trade Secretary, and I think maybe it will be sure that his diary can find enough space for me. Today."

"I really don't think…" The junior assistant secretary peered at what was written on the card. "Excuse me, but what does that say?"

"It *say* 'T. Drummond MacIntyre Two'. Tell it to Mr. Leigh."

"*Stanhope*-Leigh, it's Mr. Stanhope-Leigh…and what exactly do you want me to tell him?"

"Tell him the information that I know where this America gentleman is."

"So we really are back to square one." Arthur kicked disconsolately at a stone, sending it tumbling off towards Evren. The four of them were at the back of the small garden, out of sight and, Arthur hoped, out of Miss Renyard's mind. Quite how long it would be before she came looking for Christina and him he had no idea, but the moment she did Evren and Neyla were going to have to skedaddle pretty quickly.

"My baba say that he is doing something." Evren flicked the stone between his shoes.

"But that doesn't help us, because we *still* don't know where Trey is, we don't know where his *father* is *and* we don't have any way of getting round any more – I say, Tina, how much pocket money d'you have saved? Maybe we've enough to hire Ahmet ourselves."

"Even if we have money –" Evren hooked the stone in Neyla's direction; she took one look at Christina's delicate shoes and passed straight to Arthur – "it wouldn't be a useful thing."

"Why not?"

Evren held his hands out, palms up, and shrugged. "Exactly *where* to go?"

Arthur's shoulders slumped. "I hate to say it, old chap, but I think you're right. I quite fancied getting to the bottom of all this as well, finding out what was what and all that sort of thing…"

"Look here, Arthur…there's something I've been *meaning* to tell you." Everyone looked at Christina and she blushed, her pale cheeks almost glowing red.

"What would that be, then, old thing?"

"Because *I* wasn't at *all* tired, *not* having been out all night," she sniffed and twisted a curl round one of her fingers, "*I* got up quite a lot earlier than *you* did this morning."

"What's *that* got to do with the price of eggs?"

"I overheard something." Christina looked at her highly polished shoes. "Something I should *probably* have told you before…"

25 THE LONG ROAD

T rey had been keeping up a steady pace for the last he didn't know how long (it seemed like *hours*, but as he had no way of knowing now that his watch was kaputski, it could have been just *an* hour, or even less). The exercise regime meant that his clothes and shoes were no longer soaking wet, just uncomfortably damp, and he'd kind of warmed up. Or at least he wasn't as cold as he had been. He knew he'd so little chance of getting back to the city and finding his father that he positively *had* to keep looking on the bright side or else it was likely he would quit walking, sit down and wait to be caught.

But that was *not* going to happen.

The leather briefcase bumped against his hip as he walked (he'd thought of getting rid of it, but he was still wet enough to damage the map and possibly the gun, so it wasn't worth the risk), adding up the pluses of his situation. Choosing to ignore the very large minus that he was now quite hungry, and couldn't see much chance of food any time soon, he ticked off the fact that he hadn't encountered any more wild pigs, so far, that it wasn't raining and that there were trees lining the sides of what passed for a road. Somewhere to hide if any cars – he assumed the Germans must *have* a car and didn't fly everywhere – should come either way.

Rounding a bend in the road he saw he was about to go through the middle of a small hamlet. In the gloom he checked the map and it didn't look like anything more than a handful of buildings, but something made Trey stop and look for a way to skirt round the place. Better safe than sorry being his motto for the foreseeable future.

The unforeseen detour, which took him past a small, ramshackle building, turned out to have a silver lining.

Trey would have crept on straight past the place had one of the occupants not chosen that moment to whinny softly, the sound stopping him dead in his tracks, then sending him off to investigate. So long as there wasn't some weird Turkish animal that he'd never heard of which sounded *exactly* like a horse, his luck had just changed. With a horse he could make mincemeat of the distance between him and Constantinople!

Slipping into the stables Trey stood quietly in the darkness, breathing in the familiar scents and odours as he waited for his sight to adjust, and also to let the horses get used to the idea that someone they didn't know was there. In his mind's eye he had imagined the horses would be something like the small, sturdy mustangs Gramps had on the Topeka ranch back home, but as he finally began to make sense of the ghostly, moonlit shapes he saw that here were horses of a very different type. They were rather bigger than the ones he was used to riding, or at least two of them were, as the third "horse" turned out to be a donkey.

What had seemed like a very simple solution to his problems now took on a number of irritating complications. Like there were no saddles, as these good old boys looked like they were used to pull things, and he'd therefore have to ride bareback. Plus, of course, he would be stealing a working animal, and probably from someone who didn't have *that* much in the first place. But, because he ab-so-*lute*-ly, completely, totally and definitely *had* to get one heck of a move on, what else was he supposed to do for crying out loud?

Having discovered a fairly crude bridle made out of rope, he coaxed the marginally smaller of the two horses out of the stable with a handful of oats, promising himself that the very first thing he'd do – assuming everything went according to plan – was see that the horse got taken back home, toot sweet ("and the tooter the sweeter" he heard his gramps saying). If he made sure that happened then what he was doing was merely *borrowing*, not thieving. Which, in his book, was an excellent, not to say entirely copacetic way of looking at the situation.

"Over here, boy," Trey whispered, leading the horse across to a low fence, which he climbed up. Using the great beast's mane to haul himself onto its broad back, he grabbed the reins and geed it forward. For a second or two the horse stayed exactly where it was, but then, with a snort and a toss of its head, it moved off...

Viktor Becht had joined the *Abwehr* two years ago and had worked for Reinhardt Gessler for almost all of that time. It wasn't a bad job, except for when he was stuck in a house out in the back of beyond, in a country where no one spoke a word of German. On his own. And then, when his boss finally turns up it's with some kid for whom he has to act as a *dumm* servant. What all this business had to do with army intelligence he couldn't say, and it was definitely not his place to ask, that much he knew for sure. *Herr Oberst* Gessler gave orders – which he expected to be carried out to the letter – he did not answer subordinates' questions.

And Viktor had a *lot* of questions. There was so much going on back home in Germany, but he was stuck here in Turkey, unable to get involved in anything, only picking up occasional bits of gossip. Hardly the position for someone who wanted to be in the thick of things, catching spies, even doing a bit of spying himself. He'd be good at that; instead, here he was acting as a waiter!

Climbing up the final flight of stairs, Viktor balanced the tray on one hand, unlocked the door and pushed it open. The morning sun was streaming through a big gap in the curtains and falling in a bright slash across the bed. The boy was still asleep and the previous night's tray was on the floor.

"Wach auf! Wake u..." Viktor stopped in the middle of putting the breakfast tray down. There was something not quite right about the shape in the bed, but he did *not* want to believe what his instincts were telling him. *"Verdammt..."*

Dropping the tray with a crash, Viktor ran across the room and pulled the sheet and blanket back to reveal... just pillows. No boy. *No boy!* Whirling round he swiftly checked the wardrobe – nothing – and then moved over to the window and drew the curtains back, immediately noticing the scratched and gouged paintwork.

"Verdammt...verdammt...verdammt..."

Pushing the sash up with such force one of the panes of glass cracked, Viktor stuck his head out of the window, frantically searching left and right and left again in the vain hope that the boy was, hope against hope, still there on the roof...knowing, in his gut, that he wasn't.

"What happened, Viktor? I heard a noise..."

Viktor jerked backwards so fast he cracked his head on the edge of the window and saw stars as he attempted to stand to attention. "The boy has somehow escaped, *mein Herr*."

Reinhardt Gessler was a man used to making decisions under pressure and his mind clicked into gear, ranking the probabilities and the possibilities in order of likelihood, and what should be done about each of them. "Get out on the roof, *now*, and check that he isn't hiding...I shall go and see, if he did jump, whether his actions may have resulted in an accident." He turned to leave the room. "When you have had a *thorough* look around, come straight down. I will have the car out – I assume you have made sure to keep it in good working order?"

"Absolutely, *mein Herr*, perfect working order."

"Good." Gessler marched out of the room, leaving Viktor, who now had a dull headache, to his assigned task.

The horse had a mind of its own. While it seemed perfectly happy to go wherever Trey wanted it to, no matter how nicely he asked it wouldn't speed up faster than a fairly gentle trot. Which was, true enough, quicker than he could walk, but he had kind of imagined travelling at more of a gallop. But even though the sedate pace allowed him to occasionally consult the map as he rode, he still had no more than the *roughest* idea where he was.

The sun was now well up, which he estimated meant that it was probably around about seven o'clock and his disappearance may well have been discovered by now. If they'd *also* discovered that he'd got hold of the map (as well as the gun) then they *must've* figured he was on his way back to Constantinople. Which also meant that they might already be in hot pursuit. He had seen the odd person since dawn had broken, but no cars; so far not one, going north or south. So if he heard an automobile coming from behind him there was a fair chance it would belong to the man he now thought of as "The Enemy". It made him sound like one of the villains that the tough-but-good-guys, like Trent Gripp, were regularly pitted against. Trent *always* beat the bad guys. And so would he.

Although Trey knew he must cut a pretty strange sight, a bedraggled boy riding this jumbo of a horse, he ignored the few quizzical looks that came his way, looked straight ahead and acted as if everything was completely as it should be. While the nag trotted on at its own sweet pace it occurred to Trey that his erstwhile captors would likely assume he was on foot and keeping fairly close to the road, which pretty much followed the shoreline. So, maybe, it would be a good idea if he got off it.

Up ahead Trey saw that there was a fork in the road and thought this might to be the time to take a detour. He swung the briefcase round onto his lap, got the map out and had another go at trying to match the real world around him with the two-dimensional representation on the printed cloth, with not a lot of success. Taking another route would keep him safer, but there was a risk that, even with a map, he might get lost. Except that this race wasn't all about speed, but mostly just about getting there and not getting caught. So, if he went right at the junction, and that way still basically went south, he would eventually end up where he wanted to go. Hopefully.

Trey tried egging the horse on, pressing in with his heels again (what he would give right now for a pair of proper cowboy spurs, like he had at Gramps's ranch!), but to no avail. This animal, who more than likely spent his days hauling a plough, or something equally laborious, was obviously not about to speed up for anyone, let alone some upstart Yankee boy.

Then, somewhere behind him, he couldn't tell how far away, he heard the sound of a car being downshifted, like his father did when he was taking a corner. It was going fast, the driver revving the engine and changing back up as the way straightened out. Just like his dad would do.

It was him, The Enemy!

Trey's empty gut clenched and he felt sick to his stomach. What was he going to do? He was about to be caught right out in the open, stuck up on a horse that refused to move faster than a *snail*, and with nowhere to hide! A sense of failure, mixed with dread at what was going to happen next, began to sink through him and he drooped, his shoulders sagging under the weight of his imminent defeat.

And then, just as suddenly as the cloud had settled over him, there was a burst of mental sunshine as an idea occurred to him. Quickly sliding to the ground Trey took his shoes and socks off and rolled his trousers up to just under his knees; he then liberally rubbed his legs with dust from the side of the road. This was a *big* horse. Big enough for him to hide behind, or at least hide the recognizable top half of himself. If he played his cards right, and the horse played ball, the only person The Enemy would see, if he paid him any attention at all, would be some shoeless farmer's boy going off to work.

The car was getting louder and nearer by the second. Trey grabbed the reins and held tight, talking calmly to the horse, who was getting a tad twitchy.

"It's okay, boy, it's okay..." he whispered as he stroked the animal's neck, praying that he wasn't just kidding himself as well. "He'll be gone soon."

Trey glanced back the way he'd come and there was the car. He moved so that the horse blocked any view the driver might have of him and held his breath as The Enemy got closer and closer. Was he slowing down? Had the man spotted him? He *was* slowing down! Trey forced himself to move so he kept the horse between him and the oncoming motor...and then, in a cloud of dust, the car was gone.

It was all over.

Until, that is, The Enemy realized that he'd driven further than one boy on foot could possible have got, and came back to look more carefully.

Watched by an incurious old man who had appeared from somewhere, Trey put his shoes and socks on, rolled his trousers down and made something of a meal of remounting the horse. Kicking harder than he really meant to, he urged the animal on towards the fork in the road.

26 MORE THAN ONE WAY TO SKIN A CAT

Baba Duan sat on a really quite uncomfortable leather upholstered chair in a sparsely furnished, rather stuffy room. On the wall opposite him was a large, ornately framed portrait, a black and white photographic print of a bearded man, dressed in a highly decorated ceremonial uniform, who looked not unlike one of the old sultans – without the turban, of course. This man, whom Baba Duan knew was His Majesty George V (by the Grace of God, of the United Kingdom of Great Britain and Ireland and of the British Dominions beyond the Seas, King, Defender of the Faith, Emperor of India, as it explained underneath the picture), appeared ill at ease as he stared, pale-eyed, out of the picture. Quite often, Baba Duan mused, as he waited to be seen by Mr., the Honourable Stanhope-Leigh, being a king or a sultan was not a matter of choice but of birth; it was a job you got, whether you wanted it or not.

"Mr. Hendek?"

Baba Duan looked round at the sound of his name to see a man he'd not met before beckoning him. "Mr. Stanhope-Leigh?" he asked as he stood up.

"No, no...I'm his secretary." The man smiled, one eyebrow raised. "Please come this way, he will see you now."

Baba Duan buttoned his jacket and smoothed it down, checked his reflection in the glass covering King George's portrait, made a final adjustment to his bowler hat, and went after the man. The room he was ushered into wasn't all that much bigger than the one he'd just come from, and the man with greying temples and a dark mustache getting up from his chair behind a quite plain, leather-topped desk looked the same as any other civil servant he'd ever seen. Which was exactly as Baba Duan had expected. In Mr., the Honourable Stanhope-Leigh's business, it would pay to appear unexceptional.

"Thank you, Jenkins." George Stanhope-Leigh nodded at his secretary, who left the room. "Do sit down, Mr., um, Hendek. What exactly can I do for you?"

"For me? Nothing."

"Nothing? I see..." George Stanhope-Leigh couldn't hide his surprise as he picked Baba Duan's business card up from the desk and turned it over. "Why, then, did you ask for this to be given to me, along with the information that you knew where this *particular* person was? Why would you think *I* would be interested?"

"Because I am pretty much sure that *you* have this *particular* person –" Baba Duan made inverted commas with his fingers – "Mr. Trade Secretary. You, and not the Russian, or anyone else you might have tried to make people believe. And I also know that T. Drummond MacIntyre *Three* is missing and most probably in the hands of a certain *Herr Oberst* Reinhardt Gessler."

"You seem to know a lot of things, Mr. Hendek..." George Stanhope-Leigh got up and closed the door his secretary had left slightly ajar. "Although I thought people in your line of work normally negotiated the fee for divulging information *before* they divulged it. I don't quite understand what you want from me. In my position as Trade Secretary, that is."

"I think, here in this room," Baba Duan waved his hand rather elaborately, "you and I can understand *everything*, no? Most especially that I am not here wishing for money, or to talk to you about trade." Baba Duan sat back in his chair frowning. "I am telling you because I am unfortunately quite responsible for the young Trey being where I am almost entirely positive he is. I am not a bad man, Mr. Stanhope-Leigh, but fear I am not so good a one when threatened."

"Herr Gessler has, ah, *kidnapped* this person's son?"

"Indeed." Baba Duan took out a packet of oval cigarettes, lit one and blew three concentric smoke rings. "I am informed that yesterday Herr Gessler himself flew up to his *yali*, the villa he has taken in Rumeli Kavagi. I think I am most sure he has the boy, Trey, with him."

"And why do you think *I* have Trey's father?"

"Oh I don't *think* that, Mr. Stanhope-Leigh." Baba Duan's eyes twinkled as he smiled broadly. "I am entirely, one hundred per cent confident in this matter!"

"I see..." A look of consternation passed quickly across George Stanhope-Leigh's face, and then he returned Baba Duan's smile. "Is this matter then common knowledge in the markets and bazaars, Mr. Hendek?"

Baba Duan shook his head and pursed his lips as he tutted. "No, no, no, Mr. Trade Secretary, it is not. It is my deduction, which I have kept only to myself, until this moment."

"I do hope that is true." George Stanhope-Leigh pulled open the drawer in front of him and drew out a heavy, blue-black six-shot pistol, which he put on the desk. Its barrel was pointing in Baba Duan's general direction.

"To be sure..." Baba Duan stared at his host, aware that this was the second day running he had had a very large pistol pulled on him and briefly wondered if it was going to become a regular occurrence in his life. "It is *very* true."

"Good." George Stanhope-Leigh stood up and straightened his shoulders. "And now I think we have some work to do..."

"*We*?"

"Yes, Mr. Hendek, you are coming with me."

"I know where Trey's father is..."

"*You* know where Trey's pater is?" Arthur stared, open-mouthed, at his dainty, butter-wouldn't-melt-in-her-mouth sister. "I mean to say, how?"

The look of utter disbelief on her brother's face would, ordinarily, have tickled Christina pink, but today it didn't. Today all she felt was guilty. At first she hadn't told Arthur what she'd heard because he'd been so perfectly dreadful to her, and then, after she'd realized she *ought* to say something, the fact that she *hadn't* earlier had made it all so very difficult. She really did hate admitting she was wrong. And then everything got so very complicated, the way things can do if you don't do what you know you should.

"Why didn't you tell me?"

"Well...*because*. And I am sorry, Arthur..."

"But...!"

"Let me finish, Arthur!" Christina played nervously with one of her curls. "You see, I was up rather earlier than you this morning..."

"But...!"

"Excuse?" Evren waved his hand as he tried to attract the attention of either of the siblings as Neyla watched, bemused; at this point in an argument, in her house, there would by now definitely be some vigorous pushing and shoving.

"What?" Arthur looked like he'd forgotten anyone else was there.

"*Where* is Trey father?"

"*As* I was just *saying*..." Christina, her arms folded, turned her attention to Evren. "I was up early and I heard voices downstairs, in Papa's study, and as I went past I couldn't *help* but overhear..."

"Overhear what?" demanded Arthur.

"Papa talking to someone he called Mr. MacIntyre, that's what."

"Why on *earth* didn't you say something before!" Arthur appeared to be about to explode.

Christina looked away and shrugged. "Because you'd been beastly."

Arthur appeared to have completely lost the power of speech.

"Where is Mr. Macktire now?" Evren butted in, before he could regain it. "It is important, Christina."

"He's in the annexe; I heard Papa ask him if he was comfortable, and Mr. MacIntyre said that he was." Christina looked at the expectant faces watching and waiting. "Which is how I know where he is; but before that I heard Mr. MacIntyre asking a lot of questions about Trey."

"Questions?" Arthur frowned.

"From what I could work out, Papa had Mr. MacIntyre picked up from the hotel to keep him safe from something, I don't know what; Trey was supposed to be there, too..."

"...but was late getting back." Arthur shook his head. "He said his pa was a bit of a stickler for timing."

"Well, the fact is *they* think that Trey's *missing* – which, I suppose, he is, in a manner of speaking – but they don't know he's been captured by Russians. Mr. MacIntyre wanted to know what exactly was being done to find him; he sounded quite angry and Papa tried to calm him down. I couldn't make out *every*thing they were saying, and then I heard one of the servants coming and I had to go."

"You *spied* on Pater?" Arthur's jaw dropped.

"So did you."

"But…"

"Where is this place, this 'annexe', please?" said Evren, trying not to lose his temper because of the seemingly interminable squabbling.

"Just over there." Christina pointed to a small building behind some trees, not twenty yards away, which Evren hadn't noticed before.

"You think he could be there, still?"

"Oh I think so, I did hear Papa say that Mr. MacIntyre really must stay out of sight until things were cleared up."

Arthur looked at his sister in complete disbelief. "*How* long were you listening outside Pater's study without getting caught?"

"Oh, I don't know, about five minutes, I suppose."

"It *really* isn't fair," huffed Arthur, who always seemed to get collared by someone or other whenever *he* tried to eavesdrop.

"We should see Mr. Macktire soon, I think maybe now, yes?"

"But…" Arthur stopped mid-sentence, frowned at Evren and then nodded to himself. "No, you're right old chap, spot on. We *must* tell Trey's pater everything straight away, he'll know what to do next. Come on!"

Leading the way as if he was astride a charger in the vanguard of the Light Brigade, Arthur galloped across the lawn towards the single storey building, swiftly followed by Evren and Neyla, with Christina very genteelly bringing up the rear. Skidding to a halt in front of the door he began hammering on it with his fist, almost as if he was trying to break it down.

"Mr. MacIntyre, are you there?" he yelled.

"*Shhh*, Arthur!" hissed Christina. "They'll hear you up at the house – *and we're not supposed to know anyone's here!*"

At which point the door opened to reveal a man dressed in a crisp white shirt, a blood-red tie with dark blue pattern and a grey three-piece suit. A man whom everyone recognized from the photos they'd seen in the file Arthur had brought to Ahmet's taxi the night before. Evren, who was the only person to have actually seen the "other" man, was shocked by how much Trey's father looked like him. The resemblance was extraordinary.

"You must be Arthur, and ah, Christina, I believe it is?" said the man, with the exact same accent as Trey had; he looked slightly quizzically at Evren and Neyla, who clearly weren't either Arthur *or* Christina.

"These are our friends, and they're friends of Trey's as well, Mr. MacIntyre," Arthur explained.

"Ah, right, very nice to meet all of you." Mr. MacIntyre's smile was very tight as he slowly ran his fingers through his hair. "But I'm sorry to say that Trey is not here right at the moment, so..."

"We know, Mr. Macktire." Evren stepped forward, as if to accept whatever punishment was to come his way, as he did feel responsible for Trey *not* being there. "He has been kidnap."

"He has *what*?"

"It's true, Evren and Neyla saw it happen, Mr. MacIntyre," Arthur said. "And we suspect that a Russian who had been following you kidnapped him. And we *think* we know where he is..."

27 BULLETS FLY

Trey felt happier, even though he was still making achingly slow progress, now that he'd left the main road. However he wouldn't say he was delirious, as The Enemy was still out there and no doubt still looking for him. But, because the horse was going so slowly, this lulled him into daydreaming about restaurants and food and the *astonishing* meal (with *all* the trimmings) that he'd order and eat just as soon as he could. And, because of his lack of attention, he failed to notice that the lane he'd taken was, in fact, gently looping its way back to join the main road again.

He was so bound up in devising his perfect menu that it was more than a few minutes after rejoining the road that he woke up to where he was. And while he could blame the horse for a lot of things, this wasn't one of them. Trey pulled back on the reins and the horse obligingly stopped and began clipping some nearby vegetation, making him wish it was *that* easy to satisfy his own hunger pangs. He was just about to get the map out again when he heard the faint roar of an engine being double-declutched and around a bend a couple of hundred yards down the road came a car, its tyres squealing as they sought to keep the machine actually on the crude strip of tarmacadam.

It was The Enemy.

It had to be.

It couldn't be anybody else.

Trey's mind went into overdrive: the car was going so fast that there was ab-so-lutely *no* chance that he'd be able to pull off hiding behind the horse again. And, equally, not a hope in Hades, as Trent would say, that he'd be able to outrun it, even *if* the animal knew what the word "gallop" meant. Which he seriously doubted.

But, as he was not about to be captured without a fight, the only alternative was to get ready for battle. Swinging the briefcase round he fumbled the clasps open and took out the pistol. The pistol which, as he hastily checked, he was more than relieved to see was loaded.

He had fired guns before, target practice out on Gramps's ranch, shooting at empty bean cans and such, but this would be the first time he'd pulled a trigger in anger. And he was angry. Scared, too. This felt like such a *final* course of action, like the last thing you were ever going to do...

The gun felt awkward, almost too big and heavy for him to hold. But he *had* to do this, show these people, whoever they were, that they couldn't simply drag T. Drummond MacIntyre III off the street and expect to get away with it scot-free! Not to mention that no gumshoe worthy of the name would ever be taken without a fight. Trey raised the gun up, using both hands. The barrel wavered. He took a deep breath, steadied himself on the horse, aimed at the radiator grille of the car accelerating towards him and pulled the trigger.

Nothing...*nothing!*

It wasn't loaded?

No, no, it was the safety catch.

He'd forgotten the safety catch!

Trey pushed it forward with his thumb, repeated steps one, two and three and got knocked backwards by the force of the kick. Not to mention deafened by the bang. But with his ears still ringing, Trey had no time to think, let alone look to see where the bullet had gone, as everything started to happen at once.

The sudden loud explosion (not to mention the lump of lead whistling just inches above its head) had obviously put some much-needed vim into the nag, which reared up, nearly throwing Trey, and took off. At a speed, he had to admit, very much like a gallop. Just managing to grab a handful of mane, Trey hunched down and hung on like grim death as the horse thundered down the narrow road. In the direction of The Enemy, coming the other way. Exactly what a crash involving a large carthorse and an automobile would look like Trey couldn't even begin to imagine, except that it would not be a pretty sight.

But it never happened.

Its massive hooves ringing a dull tattoo on the uneven road, the horse sped on, right past the car, which had veered off to the left. Trey had no way of knowing whether this was because his shot had hit it, or that the driver (the bearded man he'd caught a glimpse of as he'd been stuffed in the trunk of the car) didn't want to hit a couple of tons of careening horse meat.

Risking a swift glance over his shoulder Trey saw the car being backed out onto the road again, which answered *that* question; then he saw the blond-haired passenger turning round in his seat and waving what looked like a stick at him. A puff of smoke erupted from the end of the stick, followed a second later by the crack of a pistol shot; the bullet missed, whining by like an angry hornet. Only now aware that somehow he'd managed to hold onto his own pistol, Trey fleetingly wondered if he could, like the Indian braves in the movies, fire back at them over his shoulder.

Figuring that he was going to have enough trouble just keeping from falling off, Trey flicked the safety back on and decided to concentrate on what was up ahead and save the shooting for when there wasn't an alternative. He knew he'd no chance of being able to outrun the car on the road – no matter *how* fast the horse went – and if he didn't find a way to go that the car couldn't, and soon, they were going to catch him up.

What he found, as the horse continued round the bend on its fear-driven, unstoppable, pell-mell journey, was salvation in the form of a flock of sheep about to come out of their field and onto the road. Trey galloped past, but unfortunately for *Herr Oberst* Gessler and *Leutnant* Becht, by the time they rounded the bend the animals were completely blocking the road and going at a pace dictated by the old shepherd and his even older assistant. This was meanderingly slow, and, as it turned out, something no amount of cursing, ordering, horn blaring and offers of money made any difference to.

It was quite a few minutes before Trey grasped that, while he wasn't home free yet, he'd at least been given a reprieve...

The driver pulled up outside George Stanhope-Leigh's house; he put on the handbrake, but left the engine idling. Stanhope-Leigh looked Baba Duan, sitting next to him in the back of the car, straight in the eye. "I shall only be a moment, Mr. Hendek." Opening the door he got out, then ducked back down and poked his head inside the car. "Once again, I apologize for any inconvenience, but I cannot have you loose in Constantinople, not with what you know."

"But I do assure you *most* profoundly that I would not breathe the merest syllable." Baba Duan looked at the men with extremely short haircuts and granite jawlines sitting in the two front seats. "Not one, on my departed mother's life."

"Be that as it may, Mr. Hendek, you will remain my guest for the moment."

"Guests can usually say when they go home; in Turkey, at least."

"Don't do anything stupid, Mr. Hendek, you will be home soon enough."

Baba Duan watched the man walk up the steps to

his front door, then sat back and lit himself a cigarette; he thought about offering one to the two men, but in the end he didn't. Some time after stubbing the cigarette out he'd begun to think that Mr. Stanhope-Leigh must have stopped for a light snack (it was, according to his own watch, some ten minutes before nine o'clock and therefore over two hours since he himself had last eaten, so this would be completely understandable), then the Englishman appeared at the front door with a very formally dressed older man who was, he noticed, wearing white gloves. Mr. Stanhope-Leigh's face was thunderous.

"Trouble." The man on the right looked at his colleague.

"Guvnor's *not* an 'appy man." The driver continued cleaning his nails with a small penknife.

"Best-laid plans, as they say." The first man nodded to himself.

"Very true, Jimmy. Very true."

Stanhope-Leigh got back in and slammed the car door. "I *told* the man to stay put and stay out of sight – *for his own safety*! How difficult is that to understand? Particularly as I was under the *distinct* impression we and our American cousins spoke the same language."

"Guvnor?"

"Mr. MacIntyre has gone, we know not where, Taylor." Stanhope-Leigh steepled his fingers and remained silent for a second or two, thinking. "Right!" He clapped his hands together, a decision obviously made. "Let's get a move on, Taylor – how far is it to where you say Gessler has his place, Mr. Hendek?"

"Rumeli Kavagi? I should imagine something not less than thirty kilometres, possibly? This road is not the very best, but it has not rained..."

"Take the coast road, Taylor. Fast as you like."

"Guvnor." Ernie Taylor (according to the Consulate's official listings the Trade Secretary's driver, but also a trained MI6 agent) started the car and moved smoothly away from the kerb.

"Did you bring everything, Wallace?"

Jimmy Wallace looked over his shoulder and nodded. "Got enough in the boot to start a small war, Guvnor. Just in case."

Baba Duan swallowed hard. "There is to be very much shooting?"

"Hopefully not." George Stanhope-Leigh leaned forward and got a copy of *The Times* from the seat pocket in front of him. "But, as Mr. Wallace says, it's always best to be prepared for all eventualities."

"And Mr. Macktire?" Baba Duan enquired as the car picked up speed. "What about him?"

"In this life, Mr. Hendek, if you don't do as you're told, then whatever happens will be upon your *own* head. The person I must help now is his son, if I'm not too late..."

28 LINES CONVERGE

T. Drummond MacIntyre II had been warned that this European trip was going to have its fair share of testing, not to say unusual circumstances, but being blackmailed by a gang of children was one he was sure he could never have imagined, even in his wildest dreams. But young Arthur Stanhope-Leigh, a real chip-off-the-old-block, had made it *very* clear that if he and his friends weren't allowed to come along there would be trouble. They somehow knew that he wasn't supposed to leave the grounds, and the girl, Christina, had even quoted her father's phrase – "under *any* circumstances" – word for word and in the same tone of voice.

Glancing down the street he saw the two girls, Christina and the Turkish one whose name he couldn't recall, watching him; at least *they* were doing what they'd been told. Unlike himself. That notwithstanding, if Trey *was* here in this house, surely Arthur's father would understand that he had a duty to get him back. Keeping his right hand in his jacket pocket, anxiously gripping the small Colt .32 automatic (a bullet in the chamber and ready to go, he reminded himself), he hammered on the door of the house for a second time and waited.

Still no reply.

Thinking about it, he should probably have held on for a bit. The Turkish boy had gone to get Ahmet, and it might have been better to wait for them, but he felt he'd waited long enough and that action *had* to be taken. Standing back from the door he scanned the windows, a number of which he noticed showed signs of having been recently re-glazed, and saw that someone on the first floor was observing him from behind a curtain. Then the front door quickly opened and closed behind a nervous-looking man who pretty much fitted the description the Turkish kids had given him.

Mr. MacIntyre tipped the hat he'd decided to wear,

along with a pair of dark glasses, as the nearest thing he had to a disguise. "Stanislaus Levedski?"

"Was machen Sie hier?" the man snapped, frowning tensely.

"I don't *'sprechen Sie Deutsch'*, or Russian, for that matter." Trey's father looked sideways and saw the Turkish girl, Neyla, giving him a subtle thumbs up; this was the right guy. Awkwardly he shoved the gun forward in his pocket, aiming it at the man's stomach. "Look, Mr. Levedski," he said, trying to sound a whole lot tougher than he felt, "give me back my son *now*, before I plug you!"

"Have you gone mad, Gessler?" Levedski said in a hissed whisper, a fixed grin glued on his face as he tried desperately to appear, to those he knew for sure were watching them, as if everything was just fine. *"Why are you here? You* must *go away from here* now... *Sofort* – right *now!"*

The front door opened again and a grim-faced older man, balding and wearing glasses, came out; staring at Trey's father, he spoke in hushed tones to Levedski, who was shaking his head. Without warning, the older man grabbed at Levedski's jacket and, yelling fit to bust, tried to drag him back into the house.

T. Drummond MacIntyre was a man of business, and by no means a natural Man of Action, but, with the fate of his only son at stake, something inside of him decided that now was not the time to worry too much about the differences and distinctions. Now was the time to *do* something, or he'd end up on the losing side (which was not where he *ever* liked to find himself), but just as he was about to wade in the cavalry arrived!

A horn blaring down the street, accompanied by shouts from the kids, signalled that Arthur's young Turkish friend, who had scuttled off claiming that he would have no trouble in finding Ahmet the chauffeur, had indeed succeeded in doing so. And not before time.

The car pulled up, disgorging the boy, as Mr. MacIntyre pulled the pistol out of his jacket pocket and jabbed it at the bald man's head. "Let him go!" he yelled, grabbing hold of Levedski's shirt front.

As if having to deal with a wild-eyed, pistol-wielding man first thing in the morning wasn't bad enough, with no warning at all, the man attempting to drag Stanislaus Levedski back into the house found himself being attacked by a pack of unhinged children. They punched, they kicked, and the rather dainty girl with the blonde curly hair even bit his hand; but it was the hail of stones which eventually forced the bald-headed man to retreat into the house and close the door, leaving Mr. MacIntyre and Levedski outside alone.

"Where's my son – where's Trey?" Mr. MacIntyre

growled, his nose inches away from Levedski's.

"Who is this Trey?"

"Is he in the darn house?" Mr. MacIntyre shook Levedski like a doll. "Tell me, or I'll..."

"Who *are* you?" Levedski broke in, peering at his inquisitor, the penny dropping that this man definitely wasn't *at all* whom he, even at rather-too-close-for-comfort inspection, appeared to be. This was not Gessler! So whom had they been following these last few days? And why did this person now want to know where the boy he'd brought with him, for some inexplicable reason, was? The gears in Levedski's head meshed and spun as he tried to work out what these oddest of events could mean; it took a matter of seconds, because he was a clever, if deceitful and treacherous man, for him to calculate that he was in extremely deep trouble.

Gessler, the real one, worked for the German spy service, the *Abwehr*. He, Levedski, worked for his own country's secret service, the OGPU, *and* the *Abwehr*, and it did not do for double agents to get caught. He had witnessed what could happen when one was and it wasn't a pretty sight. Ever since the first report had come in that Herr Gessler had been spotted, here in Constantinople and acting very oddly for a German intelligence officer, Levedski had been completely on edge. And his nerves were being rattled even more by the fact that his clandestine and *very* secret association with the man had never *ever* included him turning up on his doorstep!

All their communications were done through coded messages in newspapers and "dead letter drops", special places where messages, and money, could be left at designated times; the last one had been very odd, with Gessler informing him he was back in Constantinople to "sort out the problem", and that he would be up at the house in Rumeli Kavagi so there would be no more communications for a bit. No mention of what he was up to, or any boy.

From Levedski's point of view, the problem that needed sorting out was standing right in front of him: this man, who *definitely* wasn't Reinhardt Gessler, could get him killed. Or worse: tortured, *then* killed. Because his boss, Paklov, was profoundly suspicious – that was his business, after all – and in his world suspicion and guilt were often treated as one and the same thing. His boss would see he was talking to a German spy and be very quick to put two and two together. So he needed a way out, and fast. "I don't know about any boy, but I know where Gessler is, I will take you..." Levedski saw the front door open again, and he knew his time was running out. "Now, we must go *now*!"

Levedski broke away from Mr. MacIntyre and dashed

straight for the car, flinging himself into the back. For a split second it seemed as if everyone was waiting to see what would happen next: the shirt-sleeved beetle-brow who'd come out of the house frowned at Mr. MacIntyre, who sized his opponent up and made for the car himself.

Beaten to it by Arthur, Neyla and Evren, only at the last moment did Trey's father realize that someone was missing; he turned to see Christina, who was dressed more for a light luncheon than this sort of undertaking, frozen between the car and the advancing Russian. Before Trey's father had a chance to do anything (he was considering a warning shot) Evren leaped past him like a whippet, grabbed Christina's hand and had her in the back of the car so fast it was almost magical.

"Go, *effendi?*" enquired Ahmet.

"*GO!*" came a chorus of voices from the back of the cab, which took off as Mr. MacIntyre, holding his hat on, just made it into the front passenger seat.

"But go to where, if I may ask?" Ahmet changed gear and the cab speeded up.

"Mr. Levedski?" Mr. MacIntyre turned round and pointed the gun at the Russian.

"Rumeli Kavagi. There is a house."

"How long will it take?"

"It is only maybe less than thirty or so kilometres."

Ahmet answered the question as he swung the cab round a corner. "But the roads..." He shrugged expressively, not needing to finish the sentence.

"Step on the gas, Ahmet, I think that's where my boy is." T. Drummond MacIntyre II, known during his school years as Deuce, had, unlike his son, never liked his nickname. But, after this morning's exploits, he thought Deuce MacIntyre sounded exactly like the kind of fellow Trey read about in his magazines, and he had to admit he quite liked the sound of it.

Ahmet tapped his wrist. "What is the time, can I ask?"

"Just after ten to nine," said Arthur. "Oh-eight fifty-one, to be precise."

"Arthur, *really*..." Christina sighed loudly. But she let her brother's annoyingness go because she was far too excited about being rescued – *rescued*, just wait till she told her friends – by a handsome, if slightly scruffy, boy! She hadn't had such an exciting day *ever*!

George Stanhope-Leigh's driver cursed roundly under his breath. The traffic in Constantinople, at almost any time of day, was enough to drive a saint to drink, it was really. He was a man who lived by rules, and here he was, living in a city that didn't seem to have any. At least not on the roads, that was for sure. He pulled out to get past a man leading two slow, heavily laden donkeys to find the way blocked by a cart that had lost a wheel and spilled its load of hay across the road.

"When in Rome," said Mr. Stanhope-Leigh from the back of the car.

"Pardon, Guv?"

"Go up on the pavement; no one will mind a bit, I'm sure. Wouldn't you say, Mr. Hendek?"

"I think you are very possibly absolutely quite correct," Baba Duan nodded, "otherwise we will be here a lot of time. And there is no one of too much importance *on* the pavement."

Shaking his head at the foreign ways he had to put up with in his job, the driver followed orders and a couple of minutes later he was turning left onto the main shore road that lead all the way up the Bosphorus to Rumeli Kavagi.

A few minutes later, some way down the street, a taxi cab made a similar left turn and also started to drive north.

29 AN UNEXPECTED RENDEZVOUS

Why the horse finally decided to come to a halt Trey had no notion, but he guessed exhaustion would be pretty high up on the list of reasons. After all, *he* was pretty much dog-tired himself just from hanging on. So, one moment he was on the wildest rodeo ride of his life, and the next the horse was standing, its head bowed, covered in soapy sweat and with wisps of steam rising off it. This was, thought Trey as he slid to the ground, one animal which was not going to be going *any*where for quite some time. Something of a problem when you were being chased by The Enemy in a car.

Looking around (now that he was able to take in where he was, without fear of falling off) he saw there were a lot more houses hereabouts, and quite fancy ones at that. Which *might* mean that he was now actually not too far from Constantinople. But, considering the state of his ride, the only way he was going to get there was by Shanks's mare, as Gramps liked to call walking. Figuring that he'd better get the horse out of sight first, as The Enemy couldn't be *that* far behind him, he was about to lead it between a couple of houses when a car roared round the bend.

Trey panicked, not even stopping to see if it actually was The Enemy; this was possibly not the most sensible decision he could have made, but all he wanted to do was keep these men from getting their hands on him again. Dropping the reins he found a reserve of energy from somewhere and pelted down the road as if his pants were on fire, only moments later to have the car overtake him, fishtailing wildly as it came to a screeching stop sideways across the road.

Trey stopped, too. It was The Enemy.

Now that the worst had happened he was astonished to find that his mind cleared and he was able to think straight; in that moment the words of Trent Gripp came back to him: "If you can't run, the only alternative you've got is to stay and fight".

It was obvious, if you thought about it.

Trey pulled the pistol out from where he'd stuck it in his belt and aimed it at the bearded man getting out of the driver's side of the car. "Drop it!" he ordered, as the man turned to look at him, his eyes momentarily flicking down at the pistol, registering that it was one of his own Lugers.

"I do not have a gun." The man held his palms out.

"Hands up, then!" Trey stared at the man standing there, smiling at him as if they were having a polite conversation. Stared at his face, seeing the shape of it under his beard, and not quite believing it...imagining what his hair would look like if it wasn't brilliantined.

"Give that to me, *Junge. Bitte.*"

The man's voice brought Trey back. "No – what d'you think I am, stupid?"

"I do not. I think you have proved you are no *dummkopf*, so I also think that you will see that now is the time to stop this."

"Who are you?" Trey spoke before he could stop himself; he really didn't need to ask: he was the man in the pictures Evren had taken. The man who *wasn't* his father.

"Give me the gun, before you get hurt."

"Before *I* get hurt?" Trey shook his head in slightly overdramatic disbelief. *"You're* the one looking at the wrong end of a bullet, Mr. Gessler."

Trey was heartened to see that the mention of his name had stopped the man in his tracks and made him think twice.

"It seems you know somehow *far* too much for your own good." Gessler's eyes narrowed, and he snapped his fingers in irritation. "I have not got the time, or the inclination, to discuss this any further – Viktor..."

Trey began to retreat as he saw the blond man get out of the car, holding an evil-looking sub-machine gun. The thought that this was not what you would call fair play fleetingly crossed Trey's mind as he wondered if *now* was the moment when he should shoot first and ask questions later, like his personal hero, Trent Gripp. Before he could make his mind up as to what he should do, a dusty Citroën squealed to a halt, its driver leaning on his horn because the road was blocked and he seemed to be in something of a hurry to get past.

And then the weirdest thing happened...Trey heard his name being called.

He squinted at the car, the sun glinting on its windshield making it impossible to see who was inside – until Ahmet's head popped out, followed by Evren's and Christina's from behind him, and finally a man wearing a wide-brimmed hat and dark glasses appeared out of the taxi, a gun in his hand.

"Don't worry, son," the man said, in a voice that shocked Trey rigid.

"*Pops?*" Trey whispered to himself, thinking he must be dreaming, that any minute he'd wake up and find himself in his bed at the Pera Palas...until reality bit and Gessler, moving like greased lightning, roughly grabbed him, snatching the pistol. And he found himself with a barrel pressed, hard, against the side of his head.

"Let him go, Colonel Gessler." T. Drummond MacIntyre II kept what Trey could see was really quite a small pistol pointed somewhere between the two armed men he was facing, one of whom had taken his son prisoner while the other was pointing quite a *large* sub-machine gun back at him. "He's not a part of this."

"I think you will find that, as my hostage, he is," Gessler said, his grip tightening on Trey's shoulder. "Who are you, anyway?"

Trey watched as his father took off the hat that was shading his face, putting it on the hood of Ahmet's taxi, and removed his dark glasses. "T. Drummond MacIntyre II, at your service," he said.

"*Gott in Himmel!*" Trey glanced sideways and saw the blond man pointing, open-mouthed, at his father. "*Er ist Ihr Doppelgänger, Herr Oberst* – he looks just like you!"

"Quiet! Keep him covered..." Trey thought Gessler sounded rattled, but the gun remained jammed hard against his head. "Explain this situation *immediately*, or I shall shoot the boy."

All eyes were on the drama unfolding, everyone's focus on the deadly triangle. As the seconds ticked by anyone could, if they had not been concentrating so hard, have heard life elsewhere carrying on as if nothing was happening (and, this being the case, it explained why nobody noticed Arthur Stanhope-Leigh's surreptitious exit from Ahmet's taxi, or heard him slink oh-so-very-quietly behind it, allowing him the opportunity to line up his shot, take aim and fire a smooth pebble at the man with the sub-machine gun).

It was, all things considered, a cracking shot, which had the desired effect of laying Viktor Becht out cold as a fish.

As Arthur's target keeled over, his machine gun dropping to the ground with a loud clatter, Trey felt the grip on his shoulder loosen as, without thinking, Gessler turned to see what had occurred. Knowing that this was his now-or-never moment, Trey wrenched himself free, swung round and kicked out at his captor's leg for all he was worth; like the title of a Trent Gripp short story put it: *Second Thoughts Are For Losers!*

"*Kleines Miststück! Was die...*" Gessler staggered

sideways, grimacing, but aiming steady and straight at Trey, who reckoned he now knew what it felt like when your number was well and truly up.

Trey saw the man's finger tighten on the trigger... but there was no bang, no smoke, the gun did not fire. And then he realized why: the safety was still on! Opportunities, he knew, had to be taken, grabbed with both hands before they disappeared. Which, leaping forward like a torpedo, is what Trey did to the gun barrel, the element of surprise allowing him to twist the Luger right out of Gessler's hands as they both fell to the ground.

Exactly how he did it Trey wasn't quite sure, as it was all a blur, but he found himself, gun in hand and the tables well and truly turned. He made a show of pushing the safety catch to "off".

"I said 'hands up', mister."

Later, when he looked back, Trey found that he didn't really remember very much. At least not in any kind of order that made much sense. The main thing that came to mind was that his father was there, taking charge (and toting a gun!) and there was a distinct feeling that it was all over.

The next thing, after Gessler and his flunkey had

been tied up, it was like a party had started and he was the VIP guest. His father was hugging him like he'd *never* done before, his back was being patted (more like thudded) and someone was mussing up his hair; he saw faces flash in front of him – Neyla and Evren, Christina and Arthur, and Ahmet, who had a grin so wide it looked like he was going to split his face in half – and he couldn't *ever* recollect feeling so alive.

It was hard to believe, but he had done *exactly* what he'd set out to do when he'd escaped from the hotel: he had found his father! Or quite possibly his father had found him, but who was going to split hairs at a time like this?

EPILOGUE

Trey felt he was trying to do a *huge* jigsaw puzzle that had no picture on the box to help him put all the pieces in the right place. That, of course, was always the trouble when you were a kid (even one who had somehow managed to escape the clutches of a dastardly German spymaster). Because, no matter what people told you, you always suspected they weren't telling you *every*thing. And exactly how fair was that?

Not very, in his opinion.

To add to the day's surprises (from his point of view,

mainly his pop looking like he knew how to handle a gat), Arthur's father and his men had then turned up – with Baba Duan in tow – which was kind of an out-of-the-blue moment. It worked out that they'd actually left Constantinople *before* Ahmet, but there'd apparently been a puncture and changing the tyre had developed into "a bit of a job", according to the grease-and-dirt-covered, not-very-happy driver.

They'd eventually arrived to find the situation pretty much under control (Gessler and his blond-haired sidekick were trussed up like Thanksgiving turkeys, as was the Russian in the back of Ahmet's car – a guy Trey thought he recognized as one of the men who'd been following his father). He assumed Arthur's dad would be pleased that the job was done and dusted, so he was a tad taken aback when Mr. Stanhope-Leigh appeared to be less than best pleased with his father. But then he discovered that his father had not only "disobeyed instructions of the utmost clarity", to quote, but also taken Arthur and Christina with him when he left the house. *And* let them get "unneccessarily involved in his mercifully successful dealings with the Russians". Also to quote.

Considering what a twerp he'd thought Arthur was when they'd first been introduced, Trey now judged him to be one of *the* most stand-up joes he'd *ever* met –

and not simply for beaning the blond, machine gun-carrying German. He'd also tried to take all the heat, and get his sister and Trey's dad off the hook, by insisting it was all his idea that he take them with him. The guy was definitely the bee's knees!

Baba Duan had also been more than a little ticked off with Evren, but only because he'd forgotten to take his camera with him and thereby lost "the opportunistic moment of a lifetime", as he put it, to snap some possibly very historic pictures – which would no doubt have been quite profitable as well.

And while he was *kind of* interested in the ins and outs of what the Gessler character had been up to (apart from noticing that he was wearing a pretty slick false beard, he'd been too busy telling the others what had happened to him since they'd last all been together to pay much attention) what he *really* wanted to know was *how come his father looked EXACTLY like the German spy guy*? What was *that* all about, "Pater"?

But his father had so far been too busy (surprise, surprise) to explain anything to him. And so here he was, kicking his heels in the lounge of their suite, waiting to go down to the hotel's restaurant for dinner. Which was, he had to say, something of an anticlimax after all he'd recently been through.

"Trey, could you come in here a moment?"

Trey looked up from the issue of *Black Ace* that he wasn't really reading and saw his father at the study door; he dropped the magazine on the chesterfield. "Sure, Pops."

His father ushered him into the room. "Sit down, son."

Trey lowered himself into a chair, feeling, the way things seemed to be going, as if he was about to be given a serious talking-to, but for the life of him unable to think of what he might've done to deserve it. And then there was his father, sort of casually perched on the edge of the desk, which didn't quite fit the picture either...

"I think I, um...I think I owe you an explanation, Trey."

Trey looked up from examining his toecaps. "You do?"

"I know this holiday was *supposed* to be time that we would spend together, and I'm afraid it really hasn't turned out that way, has it?" Trey shrugged and shook his head. "Before we go downstairs, I'd just like to explain a couple of things about circumstances which weren't *entirely* under my control."

"Like what? I mean I *know* you've had to do the business stuff and all..."

"Well, I admit there *has* been a lot of business, but, since Paris, most of it was *not* of the kind I normally do.

You recall that rather grand place we stayed in just outside Inverness, up in Scotland?"

Trey nodded; "rather grand" hardly described it, the place was a *castle* and staying there had been something of a high point in an otherwise dull-so-far trip. I mean, the joint had swords on the walls, a couple of suits of armour and *battlements*!

"Something happened while we were there."

"What?"

"Someone I'd never met before thought they recognized me."

"You never told me that." Trey sat up straighter. "Who was it?"

"A dinner guest…it's quite possible you never even saw him. And it wasn't until we went down to London that *I* found out; as a matter of fact, it was the day you went to the zoo with the Hunter family."

"And you were supposed to turn up later, and didn't." Trey couldn't hide the disappointment in his voice; this had been an outing his father had *promised* to come on and then, kind of typically, at the last moment he'd not been available.

"I know, but there was a good reason, Trey."

"What?"

"I got some visitors, including the man who thought he knew who I was. He asked, very politely, if

'I would mind terribly accompanying these gentlemen'."
T. Drummond MacIntyre II, to his son's great delight,
pulled off a not half bad English accent.

"Which gentlemen?"

"The plainclothes policemen he'd arrived with."

"You were *arrested*! What for?"

"They had an idea I was a German spy."

The sentence hung in the air for a couple of seconds
while important bits of the jigsaw puzzle clicked into
place in Trey's head.

"Oh *I* get it! Wait a second…no I don't…if they thought
you were Gessler, who is German, why did we end up
in Constantinople?"

"I was the cat they wanted to set among the
pigeons."

"You were?"

"Sure, especially as I had been supplied with a list of
places that it would be very suspicious for a German spy
to be seen in."

"So you weren't doing business?"

"I was not, no…"

Trey left the fact that his father had been pulling the
wool over his eyes and ploughed on to the main question.
"So who the heck *is* this Gessler, Pops, and how come he
looks like you, for crying out loud?"

"That's a whole other story, Trey." T. Drummond

MacIntyre II consulted his watch. "Shall we go and eat? I've booked a table at a restaurant and Ahmet's going to drive us, I'll explain everything in the car..."

It turned out to be a one-of-a-kind journey.

After Trey's father had told Ahmet which restaurant he'd wanted to go to, he sat back, took a cigarette out of his silver case and tapped the cork-tipped end on it. "There's something we've never told you..." He took his time lighting the cigarette, then put the case and lighter away. "I'm adopted."

Trey almost fell off the seat. "*Adopted?*" His father nodded. "But..."

"Your mother and I didn't think it was something we needed bother you with, just yet...it's not like *you* were the one who was adopted. And we didn't want you thinking anything about Gramps and Gramma, like they weren't your real grandparents."

"I wouldn't..." Trey didn't know *what* to think about *any*thing, truth be told; and then the final piece of the picture came into focus. "Okay, right...so *this* is how come you get to look like Gessler, isn't it?"

"Yes, it is. My mother was German, from Hamburg."

"So *you're* German?"

His father shook his head. "I was born in Chicago,

where my mother and father had emigrated to a couple of years before; she died when I was only a few weeks old. I have always known this part of the story, but what I *didn't* know, until we arrived in London, was that I was one of identical twins."

"You mean that stinker Gessler's your *brother*?"

Trey's father nodded.

"I got stuffed in a trunk and had a *gun* jammed in my ear by my *uncle*?"

"Indeed you did. His – *my* father...*my* real father, for some reason I don't know, put one of us up for adoption and went back to Hamburg with the other; Gramps and Gramma Cecilia couldn't have children of their own, so I was the lucky guy they got instead. And they were never told I had a twin brother."

"But how...?" Trey felt a huge and quite inexplicable lump in his throat.

"How did I find out the truth?"

"Yeah..." He blinked and swallowed hard.

The car slowed and pulled up by the pavement.

"We're here, I'll tell you more when we get inside."

Ahmet got out and came round to open the passenger door, saluting smartly as they left the car.

Even though he'd already had a very large lunch (just as he'd promised himself he would), Trey still felt – even after what he'd just learned – that he could do justice to everything the menu had to offer tonight. He walked into the restaurant, taking note of what was on people's plates for inspiration. Which was why he failed to spot where they were going, and got the surprise of his life when he went through the door the maitre d' was holding open and into a private room. Everyone was there, waiting for them: Arthur and Christina with their parents; Baba Duan and Hatijeh, Evren and Neyla (so smart they were almost unrecognizable), but...

Trey stopped in his tracks. "Why didn't you invite Ahmet in? You *can't* make him wait outside!"

"I haven't, Trey," his father looked over his shoulder, "he's just parking the car."

Trey turned round to see Ahmet, hat in hand and smoothing his hair down, stepping rather shyly into the restaurant as a waiter opened the door for him. "You are the *best*, Pops!"

It wasn't long before the conversation came back round to the whys and wherefores, the who-did-this and who-did-thats of the previous few days, and it was after the waiters had taken the orders that Trey set the question ball rolling again.

"So who was this guy up in Scotland who thought he'd spotted a German spy, Pops?"

"He works for MI6, the British secret service, Trey; good man." George Stanhope-Leigh dabbed his mouth with his napkin. "He knew of Gessler – we have a file an inch thick on the man – and when he saw your father that night at dinner his first thought was that he'd stumbled onto some German espionage plot. You were under pretty close surveillance from that moment on."

"So how long did it take for you to convince them you weren't a spy, Mr. MacIntyre?" asked Arthur.

"Not long. They were able to use the new transatlantic cable service and telephone the New York office to verify I was who I said I was. Then, a couple of days later, they came to me with a proposition."

"A proposition?" Trey leaned forward.

"They'd done some digging and found out more about my adoption, and, as they said, it's not often you get handed the identical twin of a German spy on a plate. They wondered, in their slightly roundabout, but charming English way –" Trey's father smiled across the table at Arthur and Christina's parents – "if I might be able to help them out."

"I find it is astonishing what people will do, if you ask nicely," Mrs. Stanhope-Leigh said, taking a sip of white wine.

"Very true, ma'am..."

"But how could *you* help, Pops?"

"All I had to do was go about my business, as normal, but add the trip to Constantinople."

"But why Constantinople, Mr. MacIntyre?" Arthur queried. "Why not somewhere in Germany?"

"Like Berlin?" added Christina, just to annoy her brother.

"They said they'd been keeping tabs on my twin, now a Colonel in the *Abwehr*, the German secret service; they knew he was up to something down here that had to do with the Russians, and they wanted to try and put a spanner in the works."

"Which explains the places you have the inestimable Mr. Ahmet drive you here –" Baba Duan gestured with a small bread roll – "and there to!"

"You know about that?" T. Drummond II looked surprised.

"My baba know about many things…" Evren translated for Neyla and his mother and they both nodded enthusiastically in agreement.

"That he does!" George Stanhope-Leigh laughed.

As the starters were delivered Trey's father explained that, after talking things over with the US Ambassador in London, he'd agreed to help, but only if he was promised complete protection, and that neither he nor Trey would be put in any danger. Everything, he said, seemed to go perfectly, his appearance in Constantinople ruffling all the right feathers, especially the Russians.

"That man with the gun who you threw out of the—" Trey couldn't stop himself from butting in, realizing too late that this was something he *wasn't* supposed to know anything about. "I came home early and heard the shouting... I was, um, hiding behind the chesterfield, Pops, but I wasn't spying, honest!"

"Really?" Trey's father raised his eyebrows, but then smiled and decided not to pursue the matter. "As soon as I told George –" he glanced at Mr. Stanhope-Leigh – "about Mr. Paklov's visit, we knew things were coming to a boil. The man was clearly not satisfied by my story – true though it was – of me being merely an American businessman, and he sent people back to get me...the ones who I gather nearly caught you, son."

"I had also just heard from one of our agents in Nuremberg that Gessler – who had gone back to Germany only a few weeks ago – had left the city, when he *should* have been keeping an eye on some National Socialist Party rally that was being held there." Mr. Stanhope-Leigh sat back in his chair. "We thought it wise to assume he'd heard that he had been seen in Constantinople and needed to find out what was going on down here. All of which was our signal to get you two out."

"That's when our 'best laid plans' got bent out of shape, Trey, because you weren't here when George's men came to pick us up…"

"Very sorry, *effendi*…" Ahmet shrugged in a what-could-*I*-do? way.

"Not in any way your fault, Ahmet," said T. Drummond II. "Miss Renyard had told Simpson, the butler, she was taking Trey and Arthur to one place, then changed her mind; so the men sent to get Trey couldn't find him. They then went to the hotel, but, to compound matters, you were late getting back, Trey. The men assumed this meant you'd been taken straight to the house with Arthur, and so they managed to miss you again."

"But what about the blood, Pops…I found *blood* on the floor in the hotel, and a chair tipped over. It looked like there'd been a fight!"

"No mystery, I'm afraid." T. Drummond II held up his left hand, pointing to his thumb, which had a Band-Aid on it that Trey hadn't noticed before. "Knife slipped when I was sharpening a pencil…quite a deep cut, too. And they had me out of the suite so fast I knocked the chair over grabbing my jacket."

As the table was cleared and reset for the next course, Trey, Arthur and Evren (with occasional prompting from Neyla) cajoled more information out of their parents, finding out that Reinhardt Gessler had been setting up a network of double agents within the Russian secret service, and that Levedski, the man Trey's father had

had a showdown with, was one of them. The big idea had been to make it look as if Gessler himself was a double agent, at the same time as putting the wind up the Russians. As many twists and turns as a *Black Ace* story, to Trey's way of thinking – not to mention that the last couple of days had often been rather *too* close to a Trent Gripp novelette for comfort.

"Lucky for me you left your money clip behind, right, Pops? Otherwise I'd never have met Baba Duan and who *knows* what would've happened."

"Kismet!" beamed Baba Duan. "Without the help of Chance and Fate, we never all would have met and have such tales to tell!"

"I should say Chance and Fate had little to do with you somehow managing to unearth the information about the house in Rumeli, Mr. Hendek. But, however you did it, I will remain for ever in your debt for looking after my boy." T. Drummond II stood up and raised his wine glass. "A toast to you all, and with it my thanks for achieving a successful outcome!"

Trey stood up next to his father. "More by luck than judgement, as Gramps would say."

"And so he would!"

As Trey sat back down, a thought occurred to him about luck and judgement. "One thing, Pops, what about the Giovedis?"

"Who?"

"The *Giovedis*, who just *happened* to be around to rescue me in Venice. Remember?"

"Ah yes." T. Drummond II smiled. "It would have completed the picture to have Captain de Luca and Lieutenant Nicholls here as well."

"*Who*?"

"The Giovedis are actually US Special Agents de Luca and Nicholls, based in London at the Embassy; they were seconded to MI6 to look out for us the moment we got on the train to Paris. But, unfortunately, they're already back in London."

"We were on our *own* from there to Constantinople?" Trey looked theatrically shocked at the thought.

"I should say not!" Mr. Stanhope-Leigh returned the look. "A couple of my very best men took over for the last leg of the journey."

"Didn't spot them, did you, son!"

Trey shook his head. But the fact that he'd missed those two didn't take away from the fact that he *had* seen someone following them at the Gare de Lyon in Paris! Except the man hadn't been a wise guy crook, he was a good guy.

With a bit more practice, maybe he really could make it in the private detective business...

Also by Graham Marks

KAÏ-RO

Longlisted for the UKLA Literary Award

Stretch Wilson's world is a hard place. All he has, since his father was taken as slave labour, is his dog, Bone – until the fateful day when he discovers something extraordinary deep in the heart of Bloom's Mount, a gigantic pile of ancient rubbish and waste. Something that will change his life for ever.

Battle is inevitable as the sun rises on a world where once again Setekh, God of Chaos, and Horus, God of the Sky, walk the land. And now Stretch is the only person who can stop the evil that lives in Kaï-ro from taking control, for eternity.

ISBN 9780746078884

Praise for *Kaï-ro*

"With a touch of post-apocalypse adventure, a sprinkling of ancient gods, the addition of a likeable boy and his dog, and some storytelling magic, Graham Marks mixes up a novel to be devoured in one sitting."   Garth Nix

"Graham Marks just gets better and better with every book he writes."   Melvin Burgess

"There's intrigue, fantasy, violence, danger, betrayal, suspense, horror, large-scale pitched battles and revealing insights into what leads people to follow both powerful men and seemingly all-seeing gods."

The Telegraph Weekend

"A brilliantly imagined epic adventure. This is a page turner which cries out for a sequel."

Publishing News

"The battle scenes are both thrilling and moving and the characters convincingly drawn... This epic tale would transfer admirably to the screen."

Books for Keeps

Also by Graham Marks

SNATCHED!

**Shortlisted for the North East Children's Book
Award, the Cumbrian Schools' Book Award
and the Rotherham Children's Book Award**

Daniel never knew his real parents – abandoned in a
lion's cage as a baby, he was adopted into Hubble's
travelling circus. When he suffers terrible visions of
the future he desperately tries to change what he
sees. But he cannot avoid being snatched away to
London, where it seems he may have the chance to
unlock the riddle of his past. Will he like the answers
he finds?

Action-packed, filled with drama and excitement,
Snatched! takes you on a helter-skelter journey –
from the breathtaking theatrics of the circus ring to
the very real perils lurking on the streets of Victorian
London.

ISBN 9780746068403

Praise for *Snatched!*

"Graham Marks' racy prose barely lets the reader draw breath. *Snatched!* is as taut as a highwire and as much fun as a buggy full of clowns."   Meg Rosoff

"There are plenty of thrills and spills in this lively novel, and lots of richly imagined, almost Dickensian characters."   *TES Teacher*

"A rip-roaring rollicking adventure; fast moving and packed with larger-than-life characters."   *Carousel*

"The cinematic immediacy of this cracking read is entirely contemporary."   *The Scotsman*

"A gripping historical adventure...a roller-coaster ride of secret assignations, mistaken identity and kidnapping, all revealing the dark side of London life."
          Lovereading4kids.co.uk

"Well-drawn characters, good dialogue, the atmospheric background of the circus and mean London streets, plus exciting action – just the right elements for 9 to 12-year-old boys."   *The Bookseller*

"An adventure with all the necessary ingredients: heroes, villains, the circus, dangers and a happy ending."
          School Librarian

GRAHAM MARKS had his first book of poetry published while he was at art school, studying graphic design. After a successful career as an art director he decided it was time for a change and now works as a journalist and author. He has written everything from comic strips and film tie-ins to advertising copy and novels for children and young adults.

Graham is married to fellow journalist and author Nadia Marks, and lives in London with his two sons and a cat called Boots.

Find out more about Graham Marks at
www.marksworks.co.uk